THE
NURSE'S
MISTAKE

BOOKS BY DANIEL HURST

THE
NURSE'S
MISTAKE

DANIEL HURST

bookouture

Published by Bookouture in 2024

An imprint of Storyfire Ltd.
Carmelite House
50 Victoria Embankment
London EC4Y 0DZ

www.bookouture.com

Storyfire Ltd's authorised representative in the EEA is Hachette Ireland
8 Castlecourt Centre
Castleknock Road
Castleknock
Dublin 15 D15 YF6A
Ireland

ISBN: 978-1-83618-299-3
eBook ISBN: 978-1-83618-298-6

PROLOGUE

There are hundreds of nurses walking through the streets of Chicago.

I'm one of them.

But I don't belong.

It's difficult to tell though because I'm deliberately blended into the crowd, wearing a nurse's uniform like all those around me, walking in the same direction too, past the crowds that line the streets cheering us on. This parade has been organised to celebrate the work of nurses and encourage others to take up the role one day. There are children who certainly look inspired, waving at all the medical professionals as we pass by. But they wouldn't be if they knew the truth about the two dangerous nurses lurking within this parade.

There's me.

And there's my sister walking right beside me.

The sound of a helicopter buzzes overhead and dozens of police officers cast their eyes over the parade too, though not to ensure the event passes safely.

I know why they're here.

They're looking for the two nurses who shouldn't be here.

For now, we remain undetected, in the middle of the parade, keeping our heads down and trying to go unnoticed. But we are noticed when the nearest nurse walking alongside us spots the blood on my uniform.

'Nice touch. That looks really realistic,' she says to me with a smile, totally oblivious to the fact that the blood is real and the person it belongs to died only a short time ago. What's more, that body is actually a part of this parade too.

The corpse is currently lying on a gurney behind us, which is being pushed by a couple of nurses, two unsuspecting people who have absolutely no idea that the person they are wheeling along is not an actor playing an injured patient but a real, dead victim. The addition of nurses 'transporting patients' is supposed to add to the occasion and be a visual reminder of the care that these professionals give to people who need it.

But the gurney holding the body suddenly topples over and the corpse rolls onto the ground, causing everybody to gasp as they realise he's not getting up to his feet as he would be expected to, or at least groaning after taken an unexpected fall.

He is just lying motionless and, once somebody checks him, people start to panic.

That's because they are realising what I already know.

This person is really dead.

It doesn't take long for someone to scream. Then the news quickly spreads throughout the parade, like a ripple effect, the participants and the crowd only just discovering that something is seriously wrong here. But the two of us hiding among them already knew that man was dead.

We're the ones who killed him.

All we want to do now is get out of Chicago before we are caught. But the police are closing in, as is the dense crowd, and now that everyone knows there is a dead person here, that blood on my uniform doesn't seem quite so fake anymore.

My sister and I have nowhere to run.
This feels like the end.
How are we ever going to get away with this?

BEFORE

ONE

DARCY

I've been travelling on this bus for several long hours, all through the night, though I haven't slept a wink since the journey began. As I hear the brakes being applied and the large, heavy vehicle I'm on slowly comes to a halt, I could be forgiven for thinking that it's good that we're stopping. It will offer a chance to stretch my legs and get some fresh air outside. Although having a journey unexpectedly interrupted is the last thing anybody needs, let alone me, a woman on the run who cannot afford to be slowed down in any way.

But as I peer around the tall seat in front of me and get a view of what is ahead through the large windscreen, all the air leaves my body. Now, instead of anticipating a break and some food, I'm wishing I could make myself invisible.

That's because I'm seeing the things I'm trying to get away from.

Blue lights.

Uniforms.

Police.

As the bus eases to a stop a few yards ahead of the police car that blocks its route, I'm already looking around this vehicle for escape routes. There's the door I boarded this bus on in Florida several hours ago, but that's right down by the front, next to the driver. Even if he opened it for me, I'd come face to face with the two police officers who are now walking towards us. Fortunately, there's a second door at the rear of the bus, an emergency exit should there ever be an issue with the first door. I could potentially sneak away without those police officers seeing me, fleeing along the dark roadside and running into the woods that surround this bus on both sides. But as I'm about to get out of my seat to try and make my escape, a male voice speaks.

'Don't run.'

I freeze at the warning, which came from the man seated behind me. They are the only words the other passenger has said to me since we both boarded this bus. I have no idea why he spoke, or how he was able to read my mind and know that I was preparing to try and flee. And he's delayed me in my seat when I should have already been out on the roadside by now.

I go to turn around to look at him, but as I do he speaks again.

'Don't turn around. Don't even move. Just stay calm. Keep your head down. You're wearing a baseball cap. That's good.'

The mystery man behind me seems to know why it's imperative that the approaching police officers don't know that I'm on this bus, and while it is unsettling, because nobody should know my secret, he does seem to be trying to help me avoid detection.

But will his advice work?

As the driver opens the doors at the front of the bus and leaves his seat to go and speak to the officers, I do exactly as I have been told and keep my head down. The visor on my cap, and the darkness of night, means my face is shrouded from view, although things will get more difficult if the lights come on inside this bus and the officers start walking down the aisle, checking every passenger, seat by seat.

Will it come to that?

If so, how can I hope to avoid them?

Now I'm starting to regret following the man's instructions and I'm wishing I ran when I had the chance, but it's far too late. I guess I'm going to give the police, and the media, exactly what they want.

The killer nurse, in custody and ready to face her fate.

As my heart pounds in my chest, I tentatively lift my head slightly and peer out of the window to see what is going on outside. It's a risk. How do I know that one of those officers isn't about to shine a torch up at the window and look right at me at the same time as I look at him? But I take the chance anyway because the suspense is killing me and, as I do, I see the two officers chatting to the driver. The man who has been tasked with navigating this bus from the south to the north of the country, a journey of almost twenty-four hours in total, is an overweight, bald man in his fifties. His waistline tells me he has spent far too many years either sitting behind the wheel of vehicles like this or dining on greasy food at roadside restaurants; but at the moment, his biggest concern is not coronary heart disease. Rather, it's why he has been stopped from going about his business. As I see him raise his eyebrows, I'm wondering if it's because he has just been told the truth.

One of your passengers is a suspected serial killer.

I'm praying he has not been given my name, not because he'll know for certain that I'm on here. I doubt he knew who I was when I boarded, but if he does hear my name, it will most likely be followed by a request from those officers to board and search this entire vehicle. If that happens, I'm screwed. There's not enough time to make it to the rear exit and run now, and while it would be tempting to blame the guy behind me for telling me to stay in my seat, I know the truth.

I'd only have myself to blame.

That's because I am guilty of the crimes I'm wanted for.

As the tense conversation continues outside, I lower my head again, although I'm not doing it only to keep out of sight. I'm looking at the notebook in my hands, the one I've been clutching ever since this bus left Florida, because it's all I truly own in this world. The nurse's uniform I'm wearing is stolen from a hospital, as is the coat I am covering it with. My only true possession is this notebook, but that's not the only reason I won't let it leave my grasp.

It's because it is my ticket to remembering who I really am.

Written on the pages in front of me are the names of my family members as well as the address where they live. There's my mother, Scarlett, my father, Adrian, and my sister, Pippa. The family home is an address in Winnetka, Chicago. That is my ultimate destination, or at least it was until this bus got stopped. Now I'm not sure if I'll ever make it there. Though, even if I did, I have no idea if my family would be waiting for me inside the house to greet me. They might already be in police custody, and while I pray that they're still free, the odds are not in their favour. That's because I saw their names and photos on the news while waiting at the bus station in Florida, the TV screen telling me and my fellow passengers that they were wanted by the police. As was I.

Currently, I have been able to evade detection, but have they? Or are they already languishing in a prison cell, fearing for their future, or possibly trying to blame all of this on me? I wish I knew, but I'm not with them. I'm separated, the lone family member who has lost her flock, but if I'm ever to be reunited with them, I need my plan to work.

I want to leave this bus at the terminal in downtown Chicago and go to the house in Winnetka to see if there are any clues there as to where my family might be hiding. I'm hoping that they're on the run like me and, if so, I'm hoping that they left me behind some sign of where they have gone so that I can link up with them and we can keep running together. We might have to start a new life outside America, but it's a life I'd rather start together than alone. But that was the plan before this bus got stopped and, as I close my notebook and look back outside, I see something that makes my heart skip more than just one beat.

I see a police officer coming aboard.

Now I know for certain that I should have run. I start to panic before I feel a strong hand on my shoulder that keeps me in my seat. It's that guy behind me again. I thought he was helping me, but what if he's actually against me? What if he's an undercover officer who's been watching me this entire time before contacting his colleagues to come and arrest me?

I'm so stupid.

I thought I was doing well.

But now it's over.

'Excuse me, ladies and gentlemen,' the male officer says at the front of the bus, and while every other passenger is surely looking at him and his uniform, I have my head bowed and my eyes shut, waiting for only one thing.

Handcuffs.

'Apologies for the delay to your journey, guys, but this won't take long,' the officer goes on, and I think about how he's probably right. It'll only take a matter of seconds to pull me out of my seat and wrap my wrists in silver steel before I'm marched past all these passengers, pushed out onto the road and bundled into the back of that police car out there. I could fight, kick up a fuss, try to delay the inevitable, but what would be the point? Better to get this over with as painlessly as possible. I might even hold my hands up now so they can see which seat I'm in.

'As we have just informed your driver, a tree has fallen on the road up ahead and this route is now inaccessible.'

What?

'The bus will have to turn around, which will add time to your journey, but there is no other way. Apologies again and I wish you safe travel.'

I hear what sounds like the police officer leaving the bus then and, when I look up, I see the driver retaking his seat behind the wheel.

Are they kidding? A fallen tree? That's all this is about?

While a few of the other passengers around me moan and groan about the circumstances, I feel like the happiest person in the world. Never has a delayed journey felt so good. Those police officers weren't here for me after all. I'm not about to be arrested.

I'm okay.

As the engine restarts and the driver starts the tricky process of turning the bus around, I watch the police officers getting back into their own vehicle, waiting again for another driver to come along and be given the bad news. But it's good news for me and, as the bus sets off again in the opposite direction, seeking out a detour, I lean back in my seat and let out a sigh of relief. But only a short one, because then I remember the man behind me and how he seemed to know that I am a wanted woman.

I guess I should turn around and look at him at some point and, if possible, ask him why he decided to help me. Although not quite yet.

For now, my thoughts are back on my family.

The family I may still have a chance of seeing again.

TWO

PIPPA

'Mommy, I'm scared.'

Those words from a frightened child are the last thing any parent wants to hear, but that's what my four-year-old boy Campbell has said to me as he nestles in closer to me on the backseat of this car. I do my best to soothe my son by putting an arm around him and kissing the top of his head, my lips skimming his soft hair. I can feel how tense he is and it breaks my heart that I'm not able to comfort him as much as he needs me to. But I can't blame my boy for feeling the way he does. If I'm being honest, I'm scared too, and not just because we're currently travelling on a desolate country lane in the dead of night. It's because we're on the run and, if we get caught, I have no idea if and when I'll ever be this close to my child again.

'There's nothing to be scared of,' I tell my son, trying to be as brave as I hope he can be. 'Not when I'm here.'

Will that do the trick? I'm not sure, but at least we're almost where we're aiming to be.

'The sat nav says we're two minutes away,' my father, Adrian, says from behind the wheel, continuing to drive us on slowly. Even with the car's headlights beaming out in the darkness, visibility is poor. Without the navigation system, there's absolutely no way we'd be able to find our way to our destination, not only as we haven't been here before but because it really is off the beaten track. That's the whole point of us coming here though. Hopefully, we won't be found. The remoteness of where we're going should help us achieve our goal.

We're aiming to find a set of holiday cabins that were built among this national park in southern Minnesota, a five-hour drive from our homes we have left behind in Chicago. Dad heard about these cabins from a former work colleague who vacationed here many years ago, and he also recalled his colleague telling him that the cabins eventually became disused and left abandoned. We're praying that when we find the cabins, they are still in a state that allows us to move into one of them with the supplies we picked up en route. We will also have a whole national park on our doorstep to forage in, so we can lie low here for the foreseeable future.

But we have to find them first.

'Slow down a little bit, Adrian. This terrain is pretty sketchy,' says Karl, my husband, who is sitting alongside my father in the front and helping with navigation duties. It's not that Dad is speeding; it's more that the road ahead has not been travelled on for some time, so it's full of potholes, not to mention overgrown from the edges of the forest creeping in from both sides.

No wonder my son is scared. It's pitch black out there and anything could be lurking behind all the trees that surround us, if only it wasn't so dark to see them. Campbell still has his head nuzzled on my chest, deciding that he's better off hiding down there than looking around any longer, and I don't blame him. He needs the comfort of his mother at a time like this. As I look at my own mother sitting on the other side of my little boy on the backseat of the car, she gives me a reassuring look that makes me feel comforted.

'Everything will be okay,' my mom, Scarlett, says, not necessarily meaning it, but what else can she say? That we're soon to be ripped apart by the secrets and sins of our past? I'm no expert but I'm pretty sure that would be the worst thing anyone could say as the five of us continue to venture deeper into the unknown.

'What's that ahead? I see something!' my husband suddenly calls out, pointing through the windscreen at a shape that I can't quite make out in the distance. But then Dad confirms the good news.

'That looks like a cabin to me,' he says, and as Campbell lifts his head off me and takes a look for himself, I see what those in the front are seeing. There is a cabin ahead of us and, the closer we get, I see there is not just one. I count at least four, although there are more beyond them, spread around in the darkness, only it's not light enough to see those. We'll have to wait until the morning to really get our bearings here; but for now, all we need is a place to rest our heads for the night, and it looks like that might be possible, which is a huge relief to my exhausted mind.

As Dad brings us to a stop and turns off the engine, the eerie silence is almost deafening, and I feel like asking him to turn it back on so we don't run the risk of hearing something spooky. There must be animals out here, bears possibly, although it's not the wildlife that I'm wary of the most. I'm afraid we may not be the only humans around, and if we're not, our odds of staying hidden here will diminish rapidly, especially if those other people recognise us as being the people who are wanted in the news.

But, for now, I do not see anything that gives me a sign there could be other people in or around these cabins. There are no lights on in any of them, nor are there any other vehicles. It really does look like we're the only ones here, so I guess, if that's the case, all we have to do now is get out of this car and pick a cabin to go inside.

So why are none of us moving?

It quickly becomes apparent that we're all nervous about leaving the vehicle and stepping out into the darkness, never mind approaching one of the cabins and looking inside to see if anybody might be lurking in there. But somebody is going to have to be brave. Considering my mother and I are currently trying to keep Campbell calm, I'd say that task is going to fall to the two men in the front.

'We'll take a look around. You stay here,' Dad says with all the confidence of a man who feels like he has no choice.

'Be careful,' Mom quickly replies, as Karl looks back at me and our son.

'Lock the doors while we're out,' he says quietly. 'Just in case.'

'Just in case what?' Campbell asks, fear etched all over my little boy's face. Now I'm annoyed that my husband would say something to worry our son, especially when me and Mom are smart enough to have locked the doors without being told to do it.

'Everything is going to be fine,' Karl says, looking Campbell in the eyes and smiling. 'I promise.'

Again, I wish he hadn't said that last part because he can't possibly know for sure that everything will be fine, so why promise? But I know he's trying his best and, as he opens his door and he and Dad go to leave, I have to say something myself.

'I love you,' I tell my husband, but I hope it's clear that the sentiment extends to my father too and, with that said, they both leave us, shutting their doors. Mom quickly reaches forward and presses the button that instantly triggers the vehicle's locks.

The three of us in the car watch the two who are walking

towards the nearest cabin, the air filled with nervous anticipa-
tion. I see that they're taking tentative steps, as they should,
until they make it to the front door and try the handle. It's
locked, as one might expect, but that won't be an issue.

They will easily be able to break in.

There will only be an issue if there are other people inside.

I watch as my father and husband each move around the
front of the cabin, peering through a window before moving
onto the next one. As they haven't come running back to us yet,
I'm guessing they aren't seeing anything inside that warrants
panic. But they need to check everywhere. As they move
around the side of the cabin and head towards the back, I accept
that we will have to lose sight of them temporarily. But I don't
enjoy not knowing exactly what's going on, and the longer I
can't see either of them, the more my imagination begins to
torment me.

What if there is somebody else out here and they're hiding
behind the cabin?

What if Dad and Karl get ambushed? Hurt? Killed?

And what if those of us sitting in the car are next?

'I need to go and check on them,' I say to Mom, although
neither she, nor Campbell, likes the sound of that idea.

'What? No, just wait here. They'll be back in a minute,'
Mom tells me, but how can she know that? What if they're not?

'It's already been too long,' I say anxiously.

But just to be sure that it really has been a while, I wait a
few more minutes, watching the digital clock on the dashboard
progressively tick by until I can't take it anymore.

'You two stay here. I'll be right back,' I say, quickly pulling
my son in for a hug before I pull the handle on my door, which
instantly deactivates the lock from the inside.

'Mom...' Campbell says fearfully before his grandmother
tries to say she will be the one who goes instead. But I'm already
on my way. I leave the car and close the door as quickly as I can

before I chicken out of this and we end up sitting in there all night.

It's painfully quiet out here as I look around, seeing the cabin Dad and Karl went behind, as well as another one about thirty yards away and a third one beyond that. These cabins are impressive wooden structures, no doubt expensive to rent for a vacation at one time, but now totally wasted, or at least they were until we came along tonight. But apart from them, the only other thing I can see is the tops of the tall trees whenever the clouds part and a little moonlight seeps down, which isn't often.

So I get moving before fear can render me useless.

I approach the cabin and look in through the first window but see nothing, and the same goes for the second one. Then I head down the side, the same way the men went, and I'm praying that I don't get a nasty surprise when I reach the back. However, I do get a surprise, though it's nothing to do with a grisly discovery. The surprise is that I can't see Dad or Karl back here at all.

So where are they?

I almost call out to them before I decide against it, because I still can't know for sure that only they will hear it. As I look around in all directions, I start to feel even uneasier about this than I did in the car, though it takes me a few more seconds to work out why.

It's not only that I'm worried about my loved ones.

I am also getting the distinct sense that somebody is watching me.

The hairs stand up on my arms as a chill runs through me, which is not caused by the cool wind. When I look at the cabin thirty yards away, I get the feeling that it's not as empty as it seems. Before I can worry about that anymore, I hear a noise behind me and spin around to see Karl coming out of the back door of the cabin, closely followed by my father.

'It's empty,' Karl says triumphantly, then Dad explains how they were able to get inside to check.

'The back door wasn't locked,' he tells me. 'Looks like the handle has rusted and weakened the lock. But we're in, and there are beds here, so let's get unpacked and get some sleep.'

That's all good news and I hurry back to the car to not only tell Campbell and Mom but make sure they are still okay. They are, just like they are happy to hear we have access to the cabin. As we grab our things and head inside, I could almost forget the fact that the nearest cabin to us was giving me the creeps a few minutes ago.

Almost.

I look back at it one more time and, as I do, I get the same sense that I am being watched. But am I? Or is it my paranoia?

As a person on the run, maybe this is how it will always be for me now.

It must be exactly the same for my sister Darcy. I hope she stays safe.

THREE

DARCY

As I open my eyes, the first thing I need to work out is if the visions I just had of me burning a nurse's uniform were a flashback or a nightmare. I hope it's the latter, but considering flashbacks have been increasingly common for me lately, I fear it is the former. I doubt I was asleep then, simply because I'm too on edge to relax that much, so I guess it really was yet another vision of my past, the one that I have spent so long struggling to remember but is coming back to me in increasingly frequent flashbacks now.

Maybe I'll get even more flashbacks the closer I get to my home in Chicago.

It's too dark to read my notebook again, the one that carries the names of my loved ones as well as the warnings to not watch the news and never to return home. I ignored the first warning back in Florida, and the second one will be ignored when I reach my destination, but I don't see how I have any choice.

I've just killed a man called Parker in a hospital, a case of it being my life or his, so I struck before he could hurt me. I smothered him with a pillow while he was recuperating from the attack that saw me escape his basement, the nurse's uniform

I wore helping me move through the wards undetected until it was too late for anyone to stop me. I did it for a good reason – after Parker had trapped me in his basement and I'd made it out, I knew it wouldn't be over until one of us was dead. I had taken on the role of caring for his ailing father before discovering that I had put myself in a dangerous situation with Parker. It wasn't the first time my career choice of nursing had led me to a dark place, where I ultimately had to make a terrible decision. Another flashback comes, making me think that my memory might finally be returning. I see that couple again. Laurence and Melissa, him the handsome charmer who I fell for, and her his dying wife, the one I was caring for before he tried to convince me to speed up the process. My frequent flashbacks remind me that I didn't kill her, that was him. But my memories also remind me that I did take his life after that, when he threatened to take mine so that his secret could stay buried forever.

Then there's Eden, my fellow nurse and former best friend, who it turned out Laurence was involved with too. A woman who betrayed me. Although I saw in a news report recently that she is dead as well now. I don't know what exactly happened to her, but I have an awful feeling my sister had something to do with it. Pippa is better than me in every way, not just as a nurse herself but as a human being, at least that's what my broken memory is telling me. But she was dragged into my mess and maybe she's now guilty of some terrible things too. Pippa wrote these warnings in my notebook and that tells me she must still care deeply about me, as I guess my parents do too. If so, they are likely the only people in the world who feel that way about me, so I am not going to lose them without a fight.

I know it's not as simple as that though, for many reasons, and, right now, one of those reasons is playing over and over again in my mind. When I killed Parker, holding that pillow over his face and telling myself that he would have hurt me if I hadn't escaped his clutches, I was hit with a flashback of myself doing the same thing to another person in the past. I don't know who that person is, or was, but it seemed like I was in an office. There were medical books on the shelves and a desk full of papers nearby. Was it a hospital? Or was I in college? I don't remember it all now. And maybe that's for the best...

Always feeling worse whenever I spend too long with my thoughts, I snap myself out of it by looking around this dark, quiet bus. It's rumbling on through the night, on its diverted route after the earlier interception from the police, thanks to the fallen tree. My nerves are still jangling from that unexpected stop, as they are when I think about the man behind me, and how much he might know about why I'm so afraid of getting caught.

With most of the passengers on the bus asleep, and the driver way down at the front of the vehicle, fully focused on the dark road ahead, I figure this is as good a time as any to finally turn around and talk to the passenger over my shoulder.

Shifting until I can see back between the gap in the two seats, I notice the whites of the eyes of the man sitting right behind me. He's as awake as I am, and it looks like he's been waiting for a chance to talk too.

'Why did you tell me to stay in my seat earlier?' I ask quietly, my voice just above a whisper, so I can be heard above the tyres and blacktop below us but not loud enough to wake any of the sleeping passengers. 'When the police stopped us.'

'You know why,' the man replies calmly.

I do, or at least I think I do. He knows I'm a wanted woman. So how do I play this now?

'I wasn't going to run,' I try lamely, but he easily sees through that lie.

'Of course you were and I wouldn't have blamed you if you tried. But you would have been caught and you'd have already been in a jail cell by now.'

What does he want? A thank you?

'Don't worry about it,' he says, answering that thought for me. So it seems like he was doing me a good deed. But why?

'What's your name?' I ask him next, but he just smiles.

'You don't need to know that. Just like I didn't need to be sitting right behind America's most wanted woman on this bus tonight, but here we are.'

There it is. Confirmation. He definitely knows who I am.

'So, I'm guessing it's true what they're saying in the news about you,' the mystery man goes on. 'The killer nurse, responsible for several crimes, from murder to trespassing in a hospital. It's you, isn't it?'

I choose to say nothing to that, because there's little I can add.

'Don't worry, your secret is safe with me,' the man tells me. 'I don't want any trouble. I'm just trying to get home to Chicago. I'm guessing you're doing the same. My only question would be why. Why go back to the city where you're wanted the most? Shouldn't you be heading south to Mexico instead?'

I don't have to share anything with this man. I could just turn back around and try to continue my journey in peace. But I'm lonely without my family, so I might as well try and remedy that feeling by talking to the one person who I can be open with. There's also the thought in my head that, with my memory issues, he might actually know more about me at this present time than I know about myself, if he's been watching the news.

'I need to go home,' I say. 'I need to find my family.'

'You're taking a huge risk. Your luck will run out at some point.'

'I'm not as bad as they say I am,' I try to explain. 'I've been forced into doing some bad things, but that's not really who I am.'

'Who are you then?'

'I'm just a daughter. A sister.'

'A nurse?'

I nod, because I'm definitely that.

'How can someone who's supposed to help people be accused of so many terrible things?' he asks me.

'The truth is, I can't remember it all. My memories are all jumbled. But I do know one thing. I'm going to make this right.'

Our quiet conversation is halted when we feel the bus beginning to slow, and I quickly look ahead, terrified that I'm going to see the police again and, this time, they'll be coming for me. Instead, I see a bus station. It's yet another stop on this long, gruelling journey, and, as the bus parks, I notice a couple of already weary-looking travellers picking up their bags and shuffling forward to board.

The lights come on temporarily on the bus and a few sleeping passengers stir, but most just keep their eyes closed and their heads down. I decide that it's best if I keep my head down too, so none of these new passengers recognise me. As they start to get on, I pull the visor on my cap down further. I know there are plenty of vacant seats on this bus, and only a couple of people getting on, so it's a surprise when I realise somebody is sitting down beside me.

'Good evening,' says a male voice, and I'm starting to feel like my personal space is being encroached on further when this man bumps his leg up against mine and rests one of his hands inches away from my thigh. 'Are you going all the way to Chicago, gorgeous? If so, it's my lucky night.'

Oh no. While the police are the last thing I need, a creepy passenger hitting on me is a close second. But that looks like what I've got, and now what can I do?

As he places a hand on my thigh, I'm assuming this pervy passenger thinks I'll either be up for a little fun on this dark bus or too afraid to stop him trying to have his own, but as I lift my head and look at him, he sees my face for the first time. It might have been my body that he was initially interested in, but when he gets a good look at me his suggestive smirk quickly fades, and now he looks like he's sharing a seat with a ghost. He would be the second person on this bus to recognise me, increasing the odds of a phone call to the police or a social media update mentioning my name and, ultimately, reducing my chances of entering Chicago unseen.

But without saying another word, the man quickly gets up from beside me and scurries away to the back of the bus, finding himself another seat and leaving me alone like he should have done the first time.

What just happened?

As the bus starts moving again, I get it. He recognised me – but not only that.

He was afraid of me.

Maybe being noticed isn't as bad as I thought it could be.

Some people are clearly scared of me and my reputation as a killer nurse.

So I guess I have to use that to my advantage.

FOUR

PIPPA

It's not easy to put a four-year-old to bed at the best of times, but trying to do it here, in an unfamiliar cabin, in the middle of a dark forest, after we've uprooted our lives and left home all in one night? I'd say it's going to be downright impossible to get my son to sleep this evening. But, like any tired parent, I have to keep trying, and that's what I'm doing now as I stroke my son's hair and tell him that everything is going to be okay.

'Just close your eyes. I'll be right here,' I tell him, aware that his unwillingness to rest stems from how anxious he is about his strange surroundings, but I cannot blame my boy.

I look around what is now my son's bedroom. While it might once have looked appealing to vacationers who paid good money to come here and escape city life for a weekend, signs of its lack of use are showing. According to my father, it's been at least a couple of years since these cabins were used as vacation rentals, which explains the neglected appearance of this room now. Spiderwebs hang in each corner of the ceiling, a thick layer of dust covers the dressing table, and the wooden frame of this room, which was once most likely varnished and primed, looks faded and tired.

Just like me.

The cabin as a whole is extremely spacious, more than big enough for me and my family. There are three bedrooms as well as a large open-plan living and dining area, complete with sofas, tables and chairs. All of them are coated in dust too. I know Mom is out there now cleaning, particularly in the kitchen, where we hope to prepare the food we bought on our way here, but it's a big job and she'll need help. As it is, my father and husband are busy trying to get a fire going to heat this cold place up, while I'm in here, attempting to get my son to sleep, so he can stop worrying and start resting.

Wondering if the fireplace is ablaze yet, I think about how I initially baulked at the suggestion of getting a fire started when it was first mooted by my father.

'What if someone sees the light? Or the smoke?' I queried, concerned that someone could spot us from miles away and alert the police to trespassers.

'What if we freeze to death overnight?' came the curt response from my husband, and I couldn't really argue with that because it was cold. So I left them to it. I already feel warmer than I did when I first came in here, so I'm guessing the fire is roaring now, but I can't go and check yet because I still need to comfort my troubled son.

'I want to go home,' Campbell says quietly, his meek voice a reflection of how worried he looks curled up on this bed underneath one of the large blankets I took from our house before we left.

'We're on holiday,' I say to him, trying to make this seem fun, though it's anything but.

'It's cold,' Campbell replies, prompting me to pull his blanket up closer to his chin, as well as run my hands over the top of it, attempting to transfer some of my body heat to him.

'Get some sleep and we can go exploring tomorrow,' I say,

hoping that might interest him enough to close his eyes and bring the next day nearer.

'Exploring?'

'Yeah, we can go for a walk in the woods and see what we can find,' I reply, though I'm secretly hoping we don't find anything here because we're the only ones who should be in the area.

'Can we go on a dinosaur hunt?' Campbell asks, perking up, a little happier than he has been for the last few hours.

'Yes, let's do that,' I say, smiling. 'Let's see if we can find some fossils, or maybe we'll even find a real dinosaur. But one of the cute kinds who only eats leaves, please.'

'I want to see a T-Rex!' Campbell cries, and I laugh before assuring him that if there is such a thing here then we're bound to see it.

'Okay, get some sleep,' I try again. This time Campbell closes his eyes and keeps them shut.

I stay seated beside him as I wait for him to truly drift off, and when I start to hear his soft snores a few minutes later, I know he is at peace, which means I can be, too. At least as far as my son is concerned. But I'm not at peace with anything else in my life. As I leave the bedroom and rejoin the rest of my family in the living area, not even the sight of a roaring fire is enough to ease my worries.

'Not bad for a couple of guys who grew up in the city,' Dad says with a smile as he gestures to the fire, as if I could possibly miss the orange flames flickering in the room. He's clearly proud of the job he and Karl have done in getting it started, considering they are much more accustomed to living within easy reach of radiators and a central heating switch. I glance over at my partner, who is currently hauling one of our suitcases to our bedroom, while behind him Mom is still scrubbing the kitchen surfaces. We're all exhausted, we've all been busy, and for now it seems we should be able to relax. But that's not the case, at least not for me, and neither will it be when I share my concern with somebody else here. With Mom and Karl currently occupied, I decide that Dad is the poor person who will have to hear what I have to say. So I approach him by the fire, hoping the crackling and popping of the wood as it burns will make it harder for anyone else to hear our conversation.

'I'm not sure that we're alone up here,' I say to my father as I see the flames reflected back in his eyes.

'What do you mean?'

'I got a sense that someone was watching me when I was trying to find you earlier,' I go on, my voice low so Mom doesn't hear me and start panicking. 'When I was standing at the back of the cabin, I felt like someone had eyes on me.'

Dad finally stops looking at the fire and looks at me, but he doesn't seem too concerned.

'It was just your imagination running wild while you stood out in the dark.'

'Was it? This isn't the only cabin here. Why couldn't one of them be occupied too?'

'Because we didn't see any other vehicles parked around here when we arrived, nor did we see any lights on in any of the cabins.'

'That doesn't mean there's no one here.'

Dad takes a deep breath as he presumably searches for something else he can say to put my mind at ease, and I realise he is now playing the role I was just playing with Campbell.

The parent trying to soothe the worried child.

I guess it's a job that is always required, whatever the age of those involved.

'There's nobody here but us. This place has been abandoned for such a long time. I mean, look at it,' he says, pointing out yet another spiderweb. 'If anybody else was going to come here they would have done it a long time ago. But they haven't, because as you know from the long drive here, we're totally in the middle of nowhere.'

What Dad is saying does make sense, but the problem is that fear and paranoia often trumps sense, and it sure is doing so now.

'We need to check the other cabins,' I decide, though the thought scares me no sooner than I have expressed it.

'You want to go wandering around out there in the dark?' Dad asks me, a sceptical look on his face.

'Well, maybe not tonight. But tomorrow. We should have a proper look around. Just in case.'

'I suppose it's best to be sure,' Dad finally agrees. 'Okay, we'll take a look tomorrow. But it's far too late to be doing anything now other than sleeping, so get yourself off to bed and get some rest. Your mother and I will keep an eye on this place tonight.'

I feel like I should offer to stay up and help too, either with the cleaning, keeping the fire going or simply staring out the window to keep watch for the police or any sign of movement in one of the other cabins. But the truth is, I'm totally exhausted, so I know I wouldn't be any use to anyone if I forced myself to stay up any later.

'I'll go and help Karl in the bedroom,' I say before I hug Dad and then approach Mom who, bless her, is still cleaning as if her life depends on it.

'I'm going to bed,' I tell her as I open my arms out for a hug, and Mom quickly stops what she's doing and reciprocates, giving me a tighter squeeze than she would normally give me. I guess it's just because of the challenging time we're going through. But there's more to it than that.

'I have to hug you twice as hard because I can't hug your sister yet,' Mom says sadly, and my heart breaks for her. I'm worried about Darcy, and missing her like mad, but I guess the pain of missing my sibling is not quite on the level of the pain of a parent missing their child. I put myself in Mom's shoes and think about how I'd be feeling if Campbell was out there somewhere in America, totally on his own and wanted by the police, yet unable to offer him any help. That's what Mom is going through when she thinks about Darcy. I guess it's no wonder she has been cleaning like a maniac since we arrived; she's desperately trying to take her mind off it. I'm in pain too, feeling like the strong strand that runs between two siblings has been severed, and I'm desperate to reconnect it before it's lost forever.

'We'll all be together again one day,' I promise her, with no way of knowing if I can make that happen. 'And, until then, she'll be okay. Just like we will be.'

Mom's old enough and wise enough to spot a useless platitude when she hears it, but she accepts it because it's unbearable to think the opposite. With that said, I wish my parents goodnight and head for the bedroom next to the one where my son is sleeping, although I check in on him as I pass. Poking my head around the door I'm thankful when I still hear him snoring away.

I enter the bedroom that I will be sharing with Karl and see that he has mostly got our suitcases unpacked, which means he has been working almost as fast as Mom has in the kitchen. That probably means he's as anxious as she is.

'We're going to be okay,' I say, reaching out for one of his arms, but Karl ignores me and zips up one of the empty suitcases before marching it past me and putting it down behind the door.

'Hey, did you hear me? I said we're going to be okay,' I try again. But just like the first time, Karl says nothing, pretending to be preoccupied with unpacking, although he's finished now, so there's not much left for him to do. At least that's what I think until he goes to leave the room.

'Where are you going?'

'To check on Campbell,' he snaps back, finally stopping. Although it might have been for the best if he did leave because he's clearly irritated with me.

'I just checked on him. He's fine.'

'Oh, he's fine, is he? Oh good. That makes one of us.'

'Hey, what's wrong?' I ask as I go to my husband and try to embrace him, which is a stupid question and an invitation for him to snap at me again.

'What's wrong? How about the fact that we're stuck here in the middle of nowhere for who knows how long? What kind of a life is this for our son? Or us, for that matter?'

'It's just temporary,' I try, but Karl shakes his head and pulls away from me.

'This is so beyond our control that I don't even know if we should bother fighting it anymore,' he says.

'What do you mean?'

'You know what I mean,' he tells me, lowering his voice, but I don't think it's so our son won't be woken up. I think it's because he doesn't want my parents knowing that he might not want us to keep running.

'What are you saying? That we just give up and go to the police? What good will that do us? We'll all be arrested. I killed Eden and my mom and dad covered that up. And you know about it so you'll be arrested too. Where would that leave our son? He'd have nobody!'

Karl knows all this, but I've spelled it out for him one more time, reminding him of just how much is at stake for every one of us in this cabin.

Does he take it on board and give me a hug? Or does he continue to withdraw from me, placing an even greater strain on our already troubled marriage?

I get my answer when he tells me that I can have the bed in here to myself tonight, as he is going to keep watch over Campbell. Then he walks away, leaving me alone in the bedroom with nothing to do but worry.

Worry about him. About our child. About my parents. About the police. About the possibility of there being somebody else in these woods with us.

And of course, as always, *about my sister.*

FIVE

DARCY

I can see the lights on top of the Willis Tower in the distance, giving the city some colour before the sun rises within the next hour. For now it's still dark and the twinkling of the city skyline's buildings is the only light on offer. But it doesn't matter that it's not quite dawn yet because it won't stop this bus from getting to where it needs to be.

As the driver speaks into the intercom, waking up all the sleeping passengers to tell them we're almost at our final stop, I take a deep breath and clutch my notepad even tighter than I have throughout this entire journey.

We're in Chicago.

I'm back where I belong.

But is my family still here?

I stare at the buildings we're passing by, but none of them seem particularly memorable to me. That changes when I see a sign for *Greenwood Park*, and as we pass the entrance gates and I get a glimpse of the wide path that cuts through numerous tall trees, I get another flashback.

I'm walking through those gates as a little girl, holding my father's hand and skipping along, excited to be going for a picnic with my family. My mother and sister are just behind us and, when I turn back, I see Pippa skipping too. Dad is carrying a hamper in his free hand while Mom has the blanket in hers. We keep walking until we find ourselves a spot on the grass, bathed in the sunshine and with a great view of the water fountain that sits in the centre of the park.

Now, as the bus turns a corner, the park falls out of view and the flashback ends, but the warmth it gave me is enough to sustain my hopes and dreams to be reunited with my family members as soon as possible.

A few more turns and, finally, the bus comes to a stop within the boundaries of Chicago Bus Station before the driver turns off the engine and relaxes back in his seat, his gruelling work over for one more journey, at least. I'm sure he'll be back on the road again after a sufficient break, but for now he is free to do whatever he wants. Presumably, he'll sleep while the passengers around me who are rising up out of their seats and stretching have plans of their own. Some might be going home, some might be journeying on elsewhere from here, while others could be in Chicago for the very first time and hoping to start a new life in this city. Whatever their intentions, they are all taking their luggage and heading for the door, so I guess I better do the same.

As I get up out of my seat, I think about how I tried to leave it several hours ago, only to be stopped by the man behind me. Looking to him now, I see that he already has his belongings and is preparing to pass me. I wonder if he will have anything to say?

'Good luck,' he tells me, pausing for a second to wish me well. 'I'll be rooting for you.'

That's all he offers before moving on, and I watch him disembark, thinking about how he will be able to follow what happens to me next simply by watching the news. It's crazy because he could have just told somebody about me already and be on the news himself, explaining how he just travelled overnight with the nurse who everyone in America is desperate to find. But he hasn't done that. Maybe he doesn't want his fifteen minutes of fame. Maybe he can't afford to have them if he's got his own reasons for wanting to stay hidden. Whatever the case, I am eternally grateful to him for recognising me but keeping quiet about it.

But he wasn't the only one on this bus who recognised me, and I nervously look around for the man who sat next to me at a previous stop before realising who I was and making a swift exit. I spot him at the back, still in his seat and not moving, although he's looking right at me. What's he doing? Is he waiting for me to get off first? Is he that scared of me that he'd rather I went before he makes a move?

I decide to quit while I'm ahead and leave before my luck runs out, so I hurry from the bus. Once my feet are on concrete, I have to figure out where I go next. I know where I ultimately want to end up, which is the address in Winnetka that's listed in my notebook. I have to figure out the best way of getting there, though, and the best way will be where I don't risk getting recognised again.

I've not even taken ten paces outside the bus station when I see my face on the front cover of a newspaper. It must be yesterday's paper because it's blowing down the street, but it gets stuck up against a lamppost and there it is, my face, looking right back at me beneath a headline that makes my stomach churn.

CAN YOU CATCH THE KILLER NURSE?
$50,000 REWARD OFFERED BY CHICAGO PD

They're offering money for my capture now? I guess the stakes have been raised again. Now it's not only the police who have a vested interest in finding me but any members of the public who are looking to make themselves some quick cash. I wonder if the men who recognised me on the bus knew about the reward? If not, that could be lucky. If they hear about it today that could be the end of my good fortune. They might go running to the nearest police station to tell whoever listens that the nurse in the news is back in Chicago.

Against my better judgement, I pick up the newspaper and take a closer look, intrigued as to what has been written about me beneath the photo the media have chosen to use. It's an image that's clearly intended to shock the readers because, while the headline is all about a killer nurse, the image used is one of me in uniform, smiling as if I wouldn't harm a fly. I look trustworthy and professional, exactly as any nurse should, but rather than being a positive thing, the editor of this newspaper clearly wants the harsh juxtaposition of me smiling against the dramatic and almost bloodcurdling headline. As for the article itself, things don't get much better for me there either.

Residents of Chicago have been told to be on high alert as the whereabouts of 'nasty nurse' Darcy Miller, and her wanted family, remain unknown. Nurse Miller, along with her parents, Doctor Adrian and Nurse Scarlett Miller, and sister, Pippa Simpson, also a nurse, are wanted for questioning in connection with the discovery of two bodies in Lake Michigan. The bodies of Eden Carthy and Laurence Murphy were recovered from the lake and the family have connections to both victims.

Eden was sighted near the Miller family home shortly before she went missing, and a forensic search of the property proves she was there and possibly came to harm inside the house. Laurence was known to Nurse Miller as she was one of the nurses assigned to caring for his wife, Melissa, before she succumbed to cancer. It's believed that Nurse Miller and Eden had a disagreement, one that a former colleague of the pair told us was due to a love triangle forming between them and

Laurence. Now fears have been heightened that Nurse Miller
is connected to their bodies being found in the lake.

A large-scale manhunt is therefore underway to find Nurse
Miller and her family, but the police are also appealing for the
public's help.

'We are doing everything we can to find Nurse Miller and
we are confident that she will be located very soon,' said Detec-
tive Burgoyne. 'But that doesn't mean the public can't play
their part, and we are offering a sizeable financial reward for
anybody who can advise us on her location or give us information that may lead to her arrest. Please come forward if you
believe you have sighted her, and every report will be investigated thoroughly.'

As the manhunt intensifies, questions are being asked of
hospitals and medical boards all over Chicago as to how an
entire family with extensive experience in the medical profession are now at the centre of one of the biggest murder investi-
gations this city has ever seen.

I put the newspaper back down, wishing I'd never picked it
up in the first place, and I'm pleased when the wind catches it
and blows it away. I watch it flutter down the street before
whipping around a corner and it's gone, effortlessly, or at least
with far less effort than I've been exerting to try and stay on the
move. It reminds me that I need to get going again. I'm out in
the open and, while the city streets are quiet now, they won't be
as dawn rapidly approaches and millions of Chicagoans leave
their homes to start their day.

I walk quickly down the sidewalk, passing a couple of
homeless men as I go, both of them sitting in front of the shut-
ters of a disused store, one of them sleeping, the other simply
watching me walk by. Will he recognise me? He sure looks like
he could use the reward. Fortunately, I pass him without incident. Or at least I think I have.

'Hey!'

The call behind me causes every muscle in my body to instantly seize up. As I tentatively look back, I see the homeless man pointing at me.

'Can you spare some change?' he asks, and I relax when I understand he just wants my money, not the more lucrative amount on offer for sightings of me.

'Sorry, I don't have anything,' I say, breathing a sigh of relief, but only for a second.

'What about that?' the man asks me, referring to the notebook in my hand.

'This is mine.'

'Give it to me.'

'What? No.'

The man suddenly starts getting to his feet and I fear he is going to try and steal it from me, so I take off running, as fast as I can go, sprinting in a panic through the gloomy pre-dawn streets of my home city, as if I'm a total newbie here and don't belong. I don't even look back to check if I'm being chased; I just keep running until I see a taxi parked up ahead.

Opening one of the back doors and diving onto the seat behind the driver, I notice the man at the wheel startle at the sudden appearance of a new passenger. I keep my head down so he can't get a good look at my face in his mirror. All I need is for him to take me to Winnetka. From there, I can make the rest of my journey to my family home on foot.

Then maybe I'll find out what's happened to my family.

SIX

PIPPA

My eyes shoot open and my body tenses as I listen out for whatever it was that just woke me up. I hadn't even realised I'd fallen asleep, but I guess I must have, my plan of staying awake and listening out for any intruders eventually succumbing to the waves of fatigue that have been washing over me all day. I'm wide awake now and, as I look around the dark, unfamiliar bedroom, I am just waiting to hear another sound.

All is quiet, so did something wake me? Or was it just a bad dream?

I don't know, but what I do know is I'm all alone in a bed that hasn't been slept in for a long time, so there is no comfort to be found from having a person next to me, nor is there any to be found in the creepy corners of this gloomy room.

The cabin seems quiet, but too quiet. While it would be frightening to hear a creaking floorboard, it would be comforting to hear some snoring, whether it be from my son, my husband or my parents in their room. But I can't hear anything.

Not a damn thing.

I don't like it.

I decide to try and distract myself by looking at my phone. I have no signal because I removed the sim card so the police can't track it; instead I can look at photos I captured previously that have been saved to this device, and that's what I choose to do to try and cheer myself up.

I look at images of Campbell over time, from being a young baby to the bigger infant he is now, playing with toys, playing in a park or just showing me that gorgeous, wide smile of his. There are images of my husband here too, of course, some of them with our son, some alone, but in all of them his handsome smile is consistent too. Of course it is – these were much happier times.

Then I scroll across a photo of my sister and my heart breaks just as much to see her smile, because it feels like yet another beautiful sight lost to time. In this photo, Darcy is smiling as she tucks into a bowl of nachos, and I remember exactly when this picture was captured. It was when the pair of us went to a Mexican restaurant for dinner, both of us tired after long shifts at the hospital we worked at, but both holding our promise to one another that we would have a sibling catch-up over some good food. That was a fun night. It was also the last night we spent together before Darcy had her car accident a few weeks later and lost her memory, fracturing our family and sending me and my parents down every road possible to try and get her to remember.

It feels awful to think it, but as I lie here alone, miles from my real home, I consider how much easier my life would be now if I was an only child. How I would never have gotten myself into such terrible situations if I wasn't always trying to bail my sister out of her problems. She's not perfect, she's made many mistakes in her life. This time she is a victim so I've tried my best to defend her. But what if I had never had to do it in the first place? What if I had no sister? I guess things would be much simpler. Without Darcy, there would have been no dead bodies, no police, no need to flee home with my son. And no need for me to keep secrets from my husband until we reached breaking point.

It's unfair to think all of this is Darcy's fault because it's not. Laurence was a bad man who forced her to do things she didn't want to do. But the fact remains, if I had no sibling, I would be sleeping in my own bed now, next to my husband, and Campbell would be going to school today. As it is, I feel like I'm losing everything for my sister, purely because I love her and cannot give up on her.

But will it all be worth it?

The question is a stupid one. Darcy is not just my sister but my best friend, a woman who has been there for me during difficult times in my life, so it's only right that I return the favour now. Of course, none of my difficult times were anywhere near the scale of these times, but the point stands. Sisters have to have each other's backs, and I have Darcy's, regardless of where it leads us all.

Feeling like I'm losing my mind amidst the suffocating silence, I decide to get out of bed and check on my loved ones. I'm hoping they're all asleep, and they might well be, but I need to be sure.

I feel a chill as I peel back the blankets, the fire in the living area surely having been extinguished by Dad before he went to bed for safety reasons. It hasn't taken long for the cold to creep back into this cabin, and as I look for my sweatshirt to pull on, I'm thinking I might stay up now and see if I can get a new fire started myself.

I tread tentatively to the curtain and peel it back to take a look outside, hoping I won't see anything alarming on the other side of the glass. What I see actually offers me some comfort. It's a faint glow of orange on the horizon. It's dawn. Soon, this cabin and the foreboding forest it resides in will be bathed in brilliant sunlight.

I imagine I'll feel a whole lot better about things when it is.

I leave the loneliness of the bedroom behind me and go in search of some companionship, choosing to peep in the door of the first bedroom I pass, which is where my parents are supposed to be sleeping. As I look through the narrow gap in the ajar door, I see my mother and father on the bed, side by side, him with an arm draped over her and the two of them snuggled beneath the warmth of a blanket. They look exactly like a happily married couple should. Sure, they might be going through hell with their two daughters and the police investigation, but the love they have for one another endures and can withstand any test. They are an example to any couple about what it is to love and cherish the person you married. As lovely as it is to witness, I cannot help but feel more than a pang of envy that my marriage is not as solid as theirs.

My thoughts return to my husband, as well as my son, so I go in search of them in the next room. When I look in, I see my son where I left him, curled up on his bed and still fast asleep. At least he won't be exhausted today. When I look down beside the bed, I see my husband, asleep too, looking far less comfortable than our boy, but getting some rest all the same. While it's cute to see Karl sleeping at our son's bedside, I know that it's only because he preferred this option to sleeping beside me. Now, with five of us in the cabin, it seems like I'm the odd one out.

I move onto the living area and quickly spot the pile of embers from the fire earlier. Before I can even ponder how to get it going again, I rummage around for some of the food we brought with us. Mom has unpacked some of the things, though I notice she has left half in a bag, presumably in case we have to suddenly run and don't have time to pack up again. I open a bag of cookies and quickly wolf down two before I force myself to stop, not thinking it fair to satisfy my appetite when others are bound to wake up hungry soon.

While finishing my second cookie, I take a better look

around the living area than I did last night, opening a few cupboard doors, and though I don't find anything of interest at first, I eventually come across a remote control for a TV. I don't see a television anywhere in here. Where is it?

I look everywhere, but with no luck, so I'm just about to give up and assume there was one here once but it was either removed or stolen, when I find a switch on the wall behind a cabinet. I flick it, expecting it to turn a light on; instead it causes a whirring sound to start up above the fireplace. I turn to watch as the painting above the fire separates in two and behind is a TV mounted to the wall.

I quickly hit the power button on the remote, hoping I'll be able to find a news channel and get an update on Darcy and the police. The only thing on the screen is static, fuzzy black and grey, which means one thing.

There is no signal. *But there must be electricity.*

That gives me hope that we might get the TV working at some point. Having access to the news here would be a huge advantage. It would prevent the need to go out and try and get updates in a more populated area. Until someone with better knowledge than me can get this TV working, though, I can't do much with it, so I turn it off and throw the remote down on the sofa.

Pale light is filtering into the cabin now and I can hear a few birds out in the trees, chirping away and heralding the arrival of a new day. I guess the sounds will wake the others soon, so I decide to try and get a fire started, hoping they'll come in here and instantly get some warmth. Part of me also thinks that if I can impress Karl, it might make him less hostile to me today, although I am aware merely getting some flames burning does not make up for the fact we have had to flee here in the first place.

I poke around the ashes of the fireplace with a prod but there's no wood left to burn in there, and I quickly realise Dad must have found some outside. That means that if I want to get a fire going now then I'm going to have to leave the cabin and find some wood myself. But do I want to go out there alone, especially after last night's experience, when I felt like I was being watched?

I go to a window and peer out, looking towards the nearest cabin to see if everything looks as it should over there. It's supposed to be empty, so I don't want to see any lights or movement at the windows, and I'm pleased when I don't see either of those things. Maybe it was just my imagination playing tricks on me and Dad was right. We're the only ones here.

Feeling emboldened as the sun rises steadily higher and more sunlight bathes the area, I decide to put my shoes on and venture out. If this is going to be our home for a while, then it's time to start getting comfortable here.

I leave the cabin, closing the door quietly behind myself, before looking around for where there might be some easily accessible pieces of wood. I see a few chunks down in the long grass so I go and scoop them up, figuring they will do, but not quite sure. I'm totally out of my depth here, foraging in the woods.

I'm a nurse, I spend time on children's wards, caring for sick patients, taking blood pressure checks and administering injections. This is not what I was trained to do. But I already know by now that it's highly unlikely that I'll ever be allowed to go back to that line of work again.

As I try not to dwell on how much I'll miss nursing, I end up wandering a little further from the cabin than I originally intended to. When I realise, I stop and turn to head back, figuring what wood I have collected will do for now. Just before I can go, I hear the loud snapping of a branch and my entire body turns cold.

What the hell was that?

An animal?

Or a person?

I get the answer when I see a flash of movement among the trees ahead of me. They move quickly and are out of sight almost as fast as I saw them, but I get a good enough glimpse to know what it is.

It's not a deer.

It's not a bear.

It's a man.

So I was right.

We aren't alone here after all.

SEVEN

DARCY

The anxiety I'm feeling as this taxi takes me closer and closer to my family home only increases when I work out I'm not going to have anywhere near enough money to pay the driver his fare. I was already planning on getting dropped off a couple of streets away from my real destination, just to be safe, but now I feel like stopping him as soon as possible before the meter has any more money added to it. The problem is, I need to make it seem believable.

'This is okay here,' I say before I point to a house down the road. 'That's my place there. Are you okay to wait outside while I go in and get some cash?'

The driver, who doesn't seem to have realised he's been ferrying a wanted woman around for the last twenty minutes also fails to detect any problem with what I've just said, and he parks up outside the house I just indicated. Poor guy. I feel so bad just ditching him without paying after he's driven all the way out here from the city. But I have no choice. I can't pay him, so if I don't run now, he'll lock me in this car, probably call the police and then, after all this effort, I'll end up being taken into custody over an unpaid taxi fare of all things.

'How long will you be?' the driver asks me as I look at the house we've just stopped outside. I pray that nobody comes out of it who could ruin my ruse.

'Just a couple of minutes,' I reply as I try the door handle and, to my relief, it opens, so I'm not going to be stuck in here any longer.

Gritting my teeth and hating myself for fooling an innocent and hard-working man, I close the taxi door quietly so as not to disturb anybody still sleeping around here as it's only dawn. Then I start walking up the driveway to the house that I'm supposed to be going inside to get some money. But I obviously can't do that, so I head for the side gate and open it, hoping there are no nasty surprises on the other side like a dog or a homeowner who is up bright and early tending to his garden. Mercifully, there is nothing to greet me, so I close the gate behind me and now all I need to do is sneak through a few back gardens and come out further down the street where the taxi driver won't be able to see me.

The absurdity of sneaking around in people's back gardens, creeping past trampolines and climbing over short fences, or squeezing myself between bordering trees, is not lost on me. The way the media describe me, I am a dangerous woman but also a clever one, with my medical qualifications and extensive experience in nursing. Yet here I am scrambling around at sunrise like a person who has absolutely nothing going for them in life.

I guess maybe that's just who I am now.

I make it through several gardens, only setting off one security light along the way, but I didn't hear anybody call out to me, so I guess I've been unseen. Now I can sneak back out on the street. When I look down, I see the taxi in the distance, still waiting outside that house, the driver blissfully unaware that he's never going to see me again. Or at least he won't see me until he checks the news and finds out just how close he came to claiming that $50,000 reward for himself.

I walk quickly away from him, keeping my head down and my pace up until ahead of me I see the street sign that tells me I'm almost home.

Sherwood Crescent.

The closer I get, the more a few memories return to me, memories that seemed lost forever but have been flooding back to me with increasing regularity over the past twenty-four hours, which must mean my brain is finally healing, or something else is triggering them. I hope it isn't something ominous, like a person who sees their life flashing before their eyes just before they die. After all, the police want me and, if they find me, they might not take the risk of trying to capture me peacefully.

They might just draw their weapons, take aim and make sure I don't get away again.

I slow my pace as I reach the start of my street, well aware that there could be numerous police officers right around the corner, and, after taking cover behind a garden wall, I peer around it and see what obstacles lie in the way of getting home.

Sure enough, there are police here but only two of them, sitting in a stationary vehicle outside my parents' property. They are both awake, as they should be if they're on duty, but they don't seem very alert. One of them is rubbing his eyes while the other rests his head against his hand, propped up against the window of the car, both of them bored and clearly not expecting any action as early as dawn. Of course they're not. With everybody looking for them, the family who call this place home would have to be crazy to think about coming back here.

Just call me crazy.

I decide to keep the same strategy that served me so well in getting away from the taxi driver unseen, so I do my best to get closer to the house by sneaking through the back gardens of the neighbours' houses. I pass through one sprawling garden with a pool and child's swing-set in it. I'm just passing over a well-maintained lawn in the next garden when I freeze. That's because there's a middle-aged man sitting on his back decking with a cup of coffee.

And he's looking right back at me.

Even though I've clearly been spotted, I don't move a muscle, as if staying still can somehow make this man doubt what he's looking at. But I get confirmation that he knows exactly who I am when he says my name.

'Darcy?' he mutters, as if looking at a ghost, and I suppose I'm as frightening as that to the neighbours on this street who have come to know they've been living in the presence of such an infamous family as mine.

Before I can respond, he makes a sudden move to his back door, and I have to assume he's on his way to tell the officers in the police car that I'm here.

So I have to stop him before he can do that.

'Wait,' I call out to him as I give chase. As I reach his back door, I'm hoping that in his haste he didn't lock it behind him. He didn't, so now I'm in his home and, as I run through his kitchen, I'm terrified that I'm not going to catch him before he makes it out onto the street. If he alerts those police officers to my presence then not only will I be at risk of getting caught, but I'll also never get inside my parents' house to see if there are any clues as to where my family might be.

So I cannot, under any circumstances, let this man get away.

I catch up to him in his hallway where he is frantically trying to get his front door unlocked. Approaching him, I am struck by a memory of being here before, and not just before, but quite recently. I see myself standing in this hallway, my back against the wall, with my mother in front of me, preventing me from leaving, while this male homeowner and his wife stand nearby and look on.

My mother and I are arguing and now I recall what about.

I was her nurse and she was my patient. *But it was all a pretence.* She was role-playing, pretending to be ill, just to get me back in my family home and working as a nurse in the hopes that my memory might come back after my accident.

And how did I react to this news?

I ran away.

I've been running ever since.

'Stop! Wait!' I plead as I pull the man back, away from his door before he gets it unlocked and open, but no sooner have I put my hands on him than he panics and shies away from me.

'Don't hurt me!' he begs, which is a stupid thing to say, because of course I'm not going to hurt him. Then I realise that he doesn't know that. He's just believing the worst of what they're saying in the news. It's therefore going to be incredibly hard to convince him that I mean him no harm, plus I don't really have the time for it, so, with that in mind, I lean into the person he thinks I really am.

'I'll have no choice but to hurt you if you take one step outside this house,' I say as the man remains still. Now I have his attention, I need to use it to my advantage. 'I don't want to hurt you and I won't, but only if you do as I say. I need to get back inside my parents' house without the police seeing me. I just want to get something and then I'll be gone and you'll never have to see me again. Can you let me do that? Or are you going to get in my way?'

'I can let you do that,' the terrified homeowner says. But can I trust him?

'Seriously, if you alert the police as soon as I've gone, then I'll come back here and you'll find yourself a part of all these news stories next. Do you understand what I mean by that?'

He nods, his head bobbing up and down almost comically,

such is his desperation to convince me that he won't be screaming my name within ten seconds of me departing.

I have no choice but to leave now, so I go out the back door again and hope I don't hear him running out of the front. But I don't, and as I reach the boundaries of my parents' garden, I'm not hearing any commotion on the street that tells me I might be in danger.

I head for the back door once I've checked for any police officers lurking in the bushes, and the rising sun is reducing the dark shadows where anybody could be hiding. But it's also reducing my hiding spots too, so I have to be even quicker now.

As I approach the back door, I expect it to be locked and it is, which is a problem. How am I going to get inside? I should've thought this through. I can't go around the front because the police will see me. I might have to break a window.

I turn around and look at the rock pile. I'm just reaching down to pick up the biggest one when a timely flashback tells me that I don't need to be causing any damage here.

I see myself as a teenager sneaking into this back garden after a night out. I approach the rock pile before looking under the white rock for a key.

Is that key still here?

I lift the white rock and get my answer.

I pick up the key and head to the door, desperate to try it in the lock.

It slides in easily and the door clicks open effortlessly.

I'm back inside my family home. Sure, the police are at the bottom of the driveway, but for now they don't know I'm here.

I have to use this opportunity to my advantage.

What can I find here that might help me get my family back?

EIGHT

PIPPA

I was planning on letting my family have a lie-in, but not after what I just saw in the woods outside the cabin. Or rather who I saw. I don't know who that man is, but it proves that my paranoia was justified.

My biggest fear has come true.

We are not alone here.

I decide to enter my parents' bedroom first, figuring I'll wake them and tell them what I saw before I have to go in and stir my husband and potentially startle my son.

I find my parents as I last saw them, snuggled up together in the bed with Dad's arm over Mom, but their peace is shattered when I start shaking each of them and bring their silent slumber to an end.

'Mom. Dad. Wake up!' I say, my voice not as loud as it could be, but easily loud enough to penetrate whatever dreams, or indeed nightmares, they might be having.

It's my father who wakes first, rolling onto his back and frowning as he waits for his eyes to adjust to the sudden light. As he rubs his face and sees who just woke him, Mom comes alive too, initially frantic, which is understandable because of how suddenly I just woke her.

'What is it? What's wrong? Is it Darcy?' Mom wants to know, sitting up in the bed and looking like she is ready to go running to her other daughter's aid if she needs to.

'There's a man outside!' I say, putting it as bluntly as I can.

'What?' Dad cries, scrambling out of bed and going to the window. 'Is it the police?'

'No. I don't think so. I don't know who it is. It's just some guy. But he could call the police. I told you somebody else was here. I could just sense it!'

Dad pulls back the curtain and takes a look outside, but I doubt he'll see anything. Whoever it was I saw moved quickly and probably prefers to stay hidden, so I doubt they are right outside waiting for somebody to look out and wave.

'I can't see anyone,' Dad says unsurprisingly, but that doesn't make me feel any better. I've already seen enough.

'We need to leave now, before that man recognises us from the news,' I say. 'If he hasn't recognised us already.'

'Woah, slow down. We've only just got here and we don't know who that guy is or even if he's really there,' Dad says as Mom wearily gets out of bed and puts on her dressing gown, looking exhausted and as if she didn't sleep at all.

'What do you mean *if he's really there*? Are you saying that I'm making this up?' I cry, my voice getting loud enough now to wake those in the other room, but I can't help it.

'I'm just saying that you're sleep deprived and have been through a lot of stress,' Dad tries. 'Your mind could be playing tricks on you, especially out there.'

He gestures to all the trees that surround us and how, even though the sun is up now, it's still pretty murky beneath the canopy.

'I'm not seeing things that aren't there!' I defend myself. 'I saw a man. He was as real as you are!'

'Hey, what's going on?'

We all turn around to see Karl in the doorway, Campbell at his side, snuggled into his father's waist and, bless him, my son looks both sleepy and scared at the same time.

I want to tell him exactly what I just told my parents, but I fear it might frighten my boy even more, so I bite my tongue and Mom expertly fills the silence with what most mothers do best when it comes to making their family feel better.

The offer to make us all some breakfast.

Campbell likes the idea of that, so his grandmother leads him out of the room. Now he's out of the way, I can bring my husband up to speed on our latest problem.

'I saw a man out in the woods. I only got a glimpse of him, but there is someone here, so I'm telling Dad we need to go, but he disagrees. What do you think?'

It's a lot to throw at my partner considering he was still asleep two minutes ago, and he takes a few moments to process the barrage of information. But Dad has clearly heard enough, as he goes to leave the room before we can continue to debate this issue any longer.

'Where is this man now?' Karl asks nervously, and while I tell him I don't know, Dad just walks out as if there's nothing more to say, angering me, and I follow him.

'Dad, we need to talk about this,' I say as I catch up to him in the living area, where Campbell is already sitting at the dining table while Mom is pouring some cereal into a bowl and adding milk that doesn't require refrigeration, which is good because we don't have a working fridge.

'We have a TV?' Dad says when he notices the screen on the wall that I discovered earlier.

'There's no signal,' I tell him, but Dad's calm expression suggests that might not be a major obstacle.

'I'll take a look. There might be a satellite dish on the roof that just needs a little prompting.'

Really? His answer to me telling him we aren't alone here is to do some DIY?

'Am I the only one here who wants to acknowledge the problem we have?' I try, and it sure seems that way because everyone is busy with something else. Campbell is eating, Mom is preparing more food, Karl is looking to make a drink while Dad is fiddling with the remote control.

I can't believe my family at the best of times, but now, at the worst of times, they want to act as if everything is okay when it's not? I'm just about to throw my hands up in the air incredulously when Karl speaks for seemingly everyone but me.

'Where would you have us go?' he asks me calmly. 'Where else would we have a roof over our heads, and warm beds and a fire and a place to sit and eat?'

So even if my family believe me about seeing a man, which is debatable, they are not prepared to leave here, because this is the best option we have for a family on the run?

'I'm going up to the roof,' Dad says. 'Karl, can you give me some help?'

'Sure,' my husband replies, and the two men leave the cabin, possibly pleased to get away from me and my moaning, which stings more than a little.

Campbell quickly finishes his breakfast and wants to go and help the men outside, though of course he's too small to go up on the roof and do anything there.

'Why don't you take him for a walk? He could use some fresh air,' Mom suggests, as if she didn't listen at all to the part where I said there was a man out in those woods.

'What? No. It could be dangerous!' I cry, but Campbell is already excitedly putting on his shoes by the door.

'He can't stay cooped up in here all day,' Mom tells me. 'And neither can you. You'll go mad.'

The implication is clear.

I'm already going mad according to everybody else.

That's why no one else is worried about that man.

Nobody believes me about what I saw.

Maybe some fresh air is what I need, although I'm extremely hesitant as I open the door. I make sure to take Campbell's hand so he can't just run off as soon as we get outside.

'Mom, come on!' he groans, clearly eager to stretch his legs and burn off some energy, but I'll be keeping him near because I don't know where that man is and if he's still lurking nearby.

As we go outside, I see my husband standing at the side of the cabin, looking up at my father who is sitting precariously on the roof fiddling with the satellite dish.

'Hi, Grandad!' Campbell cries, excited to see the man on the roof, but I'm less so. One slip and fall and we could have a serious injury on our hands, which would not be ideal because we are miles from any hospital. Not that we could even go to one or we'd be arrested instantly.

'Be careful up there,' I say nervously, trying to push away the thought of Dad falling off and breaking a bone.

'I'll be fine. And if not, you're a nurse,' he says, trying to make a joke, but it's not funny. While I might be qualified to care for someone, it's only in the walls of a hospital where I have access to painkillers, bandages and anything else a medical professional needs for their patient. But out here, I have absolutely nothing except the simple medi-kit I brought from home, and that is hardly going to do much.

Campbell loses interest in his grandfather on the roof when he realises he has an entire forest to play in, and he suddenly pulls away from my hand and sprints off.

'Campbell! Come back!' I cry out, desperate to keep him close, but he's so fast, even with his little legs.

Before I can catch him back up, he's made it to the nearest cabin and my blood turns cold when I imagine that man being in there now, ready to grab my son and pull him inside.

'Campbell! Stop!' I beg, but he's just out of reach. We're far too close to this cabin for comfort. I have no idea if anybody is inside it and I really don't want to get close enough to find out. Just before Campbell can reach the steps that lead to the front door, he takes a fall, tumbling down and letting out a groan as he hits the leaf-covered floor.

'Ouch!' he cries, clearly having hurt himself. As I reach him, he's sobbing.

'Are you okay?' I ask, worried. But it's nothing more serious than a knee scrape. 'This is why you can't go running off without me. It's too dangerous out here. Do you understand?'

Campbell isn't happy at his bruised knee and me lecturing him, and I decide I've already had enough of being out here and want to get my son back inside.

As he gets to his feet and I take hold of his hand, I glance at the windows of the cabin, but don't see anybody looking back at me. Then I nervously look at the treeline, wondering if I might get another glimpse of that man there. But again I see nothing.

Is my family right? Did I imagine what I saw?

Or is my sixth sense correct?

It's a relief to get back inside the cabin, and Campbell is quickly comforted by his grandmother while Dad and Karl quickly follow behind us.

'Hopefully that's done the trick,' Dad says as he grabs the remote control and tries the TV again. The static has now been replaced by moving images. Dad did it. He fixed the TV. Now we're able to see the news.

But is that a good thing?

We get our answer when, after channel hopping, Dad finds a news bulletin and, as we feared, we still seem to be the top story. Or rather Darcy is. But this latest headline is even more shocking than the last ones we saw before we fled our homes.

'Darcy Miller, the killer nurse who is the subject of a large-scale manhunt, was sighted in downtown Chicago this morning.'

Darcy is back in Chicago? She must be looking for us. But how can she find us here?

I find it hard to keep my breathing steady when I understand where she must have gone.

It's dangerous, but I bet she's there.

I bet she's gone home.

But the only people she'll find there are the police.

NINE

DARCY

The house is silent as I enter it, eerily so, as if it hasn't been lived in for a while. I guess it hasn't, at least not by my family anyway. The only people who must have been in here since them are police. But they're not here now either. Apart from those two officers in the car outside, I am alone. I need to be quick because I cannot afford to be caught in here.

I close the back door behind me before looking around the kitchen and, as I do, another flashback occurs. It's a recent one. I'm sitting in here with my father, he is telling me about his wife's 'accident' and how he needs my help as a nurse. At the time I didn't know he was my father, as my memories were jumbled or lost, but I know it now and can recall how my parents 'hired' me as a nurse in a fake scenario to try and jog my memory.

I'm finally regaining a true sense of who I really am.

Being here should only speed that up.

I leave the kitchen and move through the hallway, noticing an open door and walking through into what is clearly the living area. I see sofas. A television. And a big window looking right out on the front of the house...

I quickly duck down, terrified that one of those police officers outside might have been looking in this direction and caught a glimpse of me in here. That would have been incredibly unlucky. I'll make sure to avoid getting too close to any more windows as I move around.

Next, I enter the study, and this is where more memories come flooding back. One is of me as a young girl, pestering my busy father as he tries to get some work done. The second memory is more recent. I've been caught in here, snooping through the drawers of the desk, trying to find out what I can about the people who live here. I guess I was getting sceptical of Mom and Dad and not believing the story they were spinning me about needing me here as a nurse.

It feels like so much has already happened, but I guess I don't even know the half of it, because I notice a yellow piece of tape stuck across one of the walls. It's the kind the police use when there's a crime scene.

That means something bad must have happened in here.

What was it?

Whatever it was, I guess it's why the police want to catch my family as well as me.

I look around for something, anything, that might give me a clue as to where my loved ones are, but I don't see anything and, the longer I'm here, the more I realise it was probably a mistake to come. Of course, there won't be a clue here as to my family's whereabouts. Even if my parents or sister had left something behind to help me, the police would have found it first, so they wouldn't have taken that risk.

Maybe I should just leave. Although it feels comforting to be here, as if I'm closer to my parents and sibling, certainly closer than I have felt in a long time, so I stay a little longer and keep looking, just in case.

I leave the study and head upstairs, moving quickly, aware that

I could be caught at any second. I see several doors so take the first one and it's for the bathroom. There surely wouldn't be anything of interest in here for me. I catch a glimpse of myself in the mirror, then I pause and take a longer look. This is the first time I've seen my reflection in a while and it's disconcerting. A person would usually expect to have a good idea of what should be looking back at them from the mirror, but my appearance has shocked me.

I look even worse than I feel.

My skin is pale, my hair is greasy and the bags under my eyes tell anyone who cares to look that I haven't slept properly for a while. Annoyingly, as bad as I look, I don't look different enough to the real me, the one in all the photos in the newspapers and on the news bulletins. That means I'm still easily recognisable, and that's before I even look at the nurse's uniform I'm wearing. This is the one I stole from the hospital where I killed Parker. I've kept it on for lack of anything better to wear, but maybe it's time I ditched it. However, I feel a strange comfort in wearing the uniform that ties me to my profession, so I'm reluctant to take it off. I wish I was still an ordinary nurse, waking up every day and helping people. Everything has gone wrong though, so I have to take the uniform off and find an alternative outfit.

There must be some clothes here I can change into, even if they belong to my mother, so I leave the bathroom and look for a bedroom to explore. When I find one, the master bedroom, I recall being here recently, my mother in bed, playing the patient, allowing me and my sister to care for her as if she needed it. We took her blood pressure, checked her pupils, helped her get in and out of bed. We sat with her while she ate and drank, watched old movies with her, talked to her and tried to comfort her. I thought I was doing a good job back then, but it was everyone else who was doing that. They were all acting, and I was the pawn, being manipulated, though only because they cared about me so much that they tried to get me to remember after my accident.

I feel a tear running down my cheek as I stare at the empty bed. This house just feels so cold without my loved ones in it. I shouldn't have come here because now I feel worse, and I was hardly feeling good before. A sudden dip in my morale might be the tipping point.

The easiest thing would be for me to walk out of here and just hand myself in to those police officers outside. But something deep inside me keeps me fighting on.

I know what it is.

I want to make my family proud of me.

I can't do that if they aren't around to see me so I must push on. Opening one of the wardrobes, I look for some clothes to change into, but the shelves and the hangers are bare. Everything has been taken from this wardrobe, as if whoever lives here packed and moved out.

Did the police empty this house?

Or was it my parents?

I doubt the police would have had any need to tidy away a load of clothing, so it must mean my parents packed up everything, and that must mean they had the time to plan their escape. I check more drawers and cupboards, as well as under the bed, but it's the same everywhere. Everything is gone.

While this could be unsettling, it gives me hope. My family might be okay, wherever they are. They might have enough to survive elsewhere, assuming they can get access to food. It won't be easy if they're on the news. They can't just check into a hotel, but they might have found somewhere to lie low while they wait for me to find them.

But what if I could increase the odds of us being reunited by reversing our roles. I wonder if rather than looking for the proverbial needle in the haystack, I do something that would let them know where I am? If they know I'm in the city, if they know I came here, maybe one of them might come to me.

It's a good idea, but before I can think much more on it, I hear a noise. It came from outside the house, so I quickly rush to a window and look out. I see something that sends a shiver down my spine.

It's the two police officers who were sitting in the car.

They're now walking towards the house.

I have to get downstairs before they enter or I'll be trapped in here with no escape. I sprint for the staircase, almost falling as I go but just about managing to keep myself upright. Then I take the steps two at a time, risking injury, but I have no other choice. As I return to the ground floor, I hear two voices on the other side of the front door.

They're about to come in.

I sprint to the back door, praying nobody is coming in there, and as I pull it open I think I'm just about to have a very lucky escape. But then I hear someone shout behind me and, as I glance back, I see a police officer looking right at me, from the hallway where he entered, clearly having caught a glimpse of me leaving as he came in.

We stare at one another for what feels like an age but must be no more than a second.

Then he uses his radio to call for backup.

TEN

PIPPA

The newsflash that Darcy is back in Chicago and was spotted near the bus station has sparked a fierce debate between my family members about what our next course of action should be. As such, it feels as if a divide has been created in this cabin.

'We have to go and find her,' I cry, not seeing how there could be any other possible alternative. 'She must be looking for us, but she'll never find us here. She needs our help!'

'We can't take that risk,' Karl snaps back. 'We're safe here, but not if we go back to the city. What good will it do if we're all caught?'

'So you just want to leave her on her own?' I ask, aghast, upset that my husband is not seeing this how I do, but also not surprised, because we've been on different pages since all this began.

'How would we even find her? She could be anywhere in Chicago. We wouldn't know where to look!'

'Yes, we would. She'll go home. Back to the house. She has the address in the notebook I gave her. That's where she'll be.'

'Then she'll be arrested!'

Karl is not backing down, but neither am I, and I turn to my parents to get their thoughts, although the fact that neither of them have been vocally backing me yet makes me nervous.

'Mom. Dad. We have to go and help Darcy. Right?'

'Of course,' Mom says, which is promising, but Dad is shaking his head.

'No. We can't all go. Karl is right. It's too risky. If we all get caught then it's over.'

'Okay, I'll just go,' I say, but while that sounded simple in my head, it's much more difficult in reality, and I only have to look at my son to see what I stand to lose if it goes wrong.

'Can I come?' Campbell asks me, not understanding the severity of the situation and probably thinking this is just another adventure. 'I want to go home. I don't like it here.'

'No, you're staying here,' Karl says, and I have to agree with my husband on that one. Our son has to stay here. He'd only make finding Darcy harder.

'She must be so afraid,' Mom says sadly as she continues to watch the news. 'So confused. My poor girl.'

'I will go and look for her,' Dad says, not looking like he feels confident about how that plan will pan out, but that he has to try anyway. I feel a strong urge to be the one to go, like I will have the best odds of success, although there's no way of knowing that for sure because there are far too many variables at play. Whoever goes, they could be spotted and arrested long before they get back to the city, so even debating what to do might be a waste of time.

'I can find her,' I say, trying to sound more confident than Dad, but Karl just shakes his head.

'That's right. Abandon your family *again*.'

'Excuse me?'

'You've got a husband and son here, yet off you want to go, trying to save your sister yet again. When are you ever going to stop trying to bail her out and put us first?'

I'm hurt that Karl would voice such an opinion in front of

everyone else, especially Campbell. He doesn't need to hear us argue, so I bite my tongue before telling my son to go to his bedroom.

Campbell sulks and moans but eventually goes, and that's for the best because at least he won't get upset by whatever may be said next.

'How dare you say such a thing,' I tell Karl. 'I'm trying my best here.'

'No, you're trying to do what's best for Darcy. That's not what's best for us. She got us all into this mess, so let her deal with the police. She isn't here, trying to save us, is she? So why should we be trying to save her?'

'Because she doesn't have anybody else!'

'Okay, everybody just try and calm down,' Dad says as Mom starts to get upset, and I wish I'd sent her to the bedroom too. 'There's nothing on the news about Darcy being caught, just seen. So we have to assume she's still okay for now. That gives us some time.'

'We don't know how she is. Her memory issues. She might be having flashbacks or she might be getting more confused,' Mom says miserably, so I try to add some optimism.

'The fact she made it to Chicago shows she's thinking clearly,' I say. 'She wouldn't have made it that far if she was struggling.'

'I'm sick of talking about this,' Karl adds. 'I was the one who said it was a bad idea to run in the first place. Yet here we are. Now you all want to go back? We should have done the right thing a long time ago and just told the police the truth. That Darcy started all this and everything that has happened since has been us trying to cover for her.'

It's a risky strategy for my husband to choose, to actively say this is all on Darcy when he's with her parents, because they are always going to defend and love her more than him, but he's clearly exhausted and past the point of wanting to keep doing this. I can't blame him for part of that, I'm exhausted too. But there's no way we can just go to the police now. It's way beyond that.

Before we can debate any further, we're suddenly interrupted by another newsflash.

'We're getting reports that Nurse Miller, the subject of a huge manhunt, has just been spotted at an address in Winnetka.'

My heart starts thudding – Darcy really has gone home. But has she been caught?

My parents and I collectively hold our breaths as we watch the news for more updates, but Karl has clearly had enough of all our lives hinging on the actions of my sister. He leaves the room, telling me he's going to check on Campbell. I should go and do the same, but I just need to make sure Darcy has not been caught yet, and according to this latest news report, the police were very close to catching her before she fled the house.

'He's gone!'

The panicked voice from behind us causes us all to look away from the TV. Karl is rushing back into the living area with a flustered look on his face. 'Campbell! He's not in his bedroom! The window's open! He's gone!'

My parents quickly check the other rooms but there is no sign of their grandson, forcing Karl to go to the door. I quickly follow him. Both of us are desperate to get outside and catch our son before he gets too far, but can we do it? As we run outside, we look in all directions for him, but there is no sign of the little boy, and this situation is just going from bad to worse.

This is all our fault. We raised our voices in front of him. He heard us arguing, saw how angry we were, and thought it had something to do with him. So he did what any young child would do and blamed himself, even though that's totally wrong. *And now he's gone.*

I'm gripped by fear as I think about my son lost in this forest, how he could be anywhere, in any direction, getting further away from us and never being able to find his way back. I think about what might happen if he falls, gets injured, stuck somewhere. Or if he encounters a dangerous wild animal who mistakes him for prey. Then I think about that man I saw earlier.

What if he finds my son before I do?

'We need to split up!' I decide as my parents join us in looking around at the dense forest that is obscuring our view of the boy we love so much.

'I'll go this way!' I cry, picking what I feel is the most logical route Campbell might have taken from the bedroom window he climbed out of, and running in that direction as fast as I can.

'Campbell!' I call out, but the only things I hear are the rest of my family members shouting the same name as they go off in opposite directions. We spread out and their cries get quieter until the only voice I can hear is my own. Now I'm deep in the forest with only myself and hundreds of trees, and I'm scared.

I'm really, really scared.

Then I hear something.

It's a faint cry, distant, but one I recognise instantly as belonging to my son.

'Campbell!'

I run towards the sound of the cry, afraid of what might have caused it, relieved too that I might have just narrowed down the area where he could be. And then I see him, lying on the forest floor among all sorts of foliage.

Except he's not alone.

A man is with him.

It's the man I saw earlier.

He wasn't a figment of my imagination like everyone else thought he was.

He is very, very real.

Now he's got my son.

And there is blood on the man's hands.

'What are you doing? Get away from him!' I cry as I approach, and the man looks startled when he sees me rushing towards him, probably looking like I'm ready to attack. He quickly regains his composure and holds up his hands to show that he isn't actually doing anything to harm my boy, who is lying before him with a pained expression on his face.

'I just found him out here. He's hurt but he's okay,' the man says as I reach Campbell and instantly begin making checks on him.

'What happened? What did you do?' I ask him and my son, firing questions at them both that are far too frequent to all be answered, but it's the adrenaline.

'Be careful,' the man says, as if I would ever do anything to hurt my son, but maybe he just assumes I'm going to be clumsy.

'I'm a nurse!' I snap back to make it clear that I'm more than qualified to take charge now, regardless of my relationship to the injured party.

Making a visual check, I see blood on Campbell's leg, as well as note his trousers are torn.

'He's cut himself,' the man says to me before pointing to the sharp end of a branch that protrudes from a nearby tree. 'I'm guessing it was on that.'

It seems the man is right, my son does have a leg wound consistent with what could be a cut from that tree. There's a lot of blood but I can't assess the wound properly until I've cleared it up and disinfected the injured area. That's not exactly something that can be done out here and, depending on the severity of the injury, it could require a doctor to look at it in a hospital. However, if we go there, that would be the time when this is all over for us.

But if my son needs medical help, I will not put my own needs in front of his, and I'm hoping that with my own medical training, his injury might be one I can help remedy myself.

The mystery man has taken a step back to give me more

space, but I still have no idea who he is or if he represents a threat.

How do I even know he's not the one who hurt my son?

The only way I would know for sure would be if Campbell told me, but he's still too upset, plus he might not say if he's afraid. That's why I have to push my worries about this man to the back of my mind and focus on getting Campbell somewhere more comfortable.

'We need to get you back to the cabin,' I say to my son as he continues to whimper. 'It's going to hurt, but I need you to be brave.'

'Ouch!' Campbell says as I try to lift him, and I guess his leg is even more badly hurt than I thought if he can't put weight on it. Or maybe it's the shock of the accident making him want to stay still. Either way, he can't walk.

'I'll help you,' the man says, and I'm in no position to refuse that offer. It's not going to be easy getting Campbell back by myself, especially in difficult terrain, and then there's the fact that I was running through here so frantically that I'm not even sure of the correct way back to the cabin.

I lift my son up, hearing him groan, and his little body clings to me as he wraps his arms around my neck. He's heavy, but I could hold him for a little while, although all the way back? I'm not so sure. I start moving when the man directs the way to go.

'This way,' he says, pointing through the trees, so I quickly follow him, with little choice but to trust him because I'm lost and time is of the essence. But even moving quickly, Campbell is awkward to hold, and I'm worried about tripping and falling over, injuring my son further.

'Here. Let me carry him,' the man offers, aware of my struggle.

'No. I'm fine,' I try, but it becomes obvious that's a lie when I almost lose my footing a second later.

'Come on. We'll be quicker if I carry him,' the man urges, and he beckons me to pass Campbell to him.

Should I do it?

I wish my husband was here to help, or either of my parents. But it's just me or him.

What do I do?

ELEVEN

DARCY

I'm running as fast as I can while trying to stay hidden. Behind me, I hear sirens from the police cars racing to the house from where I've just fled.

That was so close, I could have been caught then and this would have all been over. I've got away and I'm still free, though for how long I have no idea. The police will know I'm back in Chicago now, and they'll know I'm on foot in the area, which means they have a very good chance of catching me, especially if they send up a helicopter.

I need to get into the city as quickly as possible, to where it's busy, where there's more hiding places and more people to hide among. I see a group of people at a bus stop up ahead and, while my initial thought is to avoid them, I realise I'm not going to last very long out here on my own in the suburbs. I'm going to have to take a chance, so I join the back of the line at the bus stop and pray our transport will be along shortly.

I keep my head down and everyone else is doing the same thing, most of them lost in their mobile phones, although one man is reading a newspaper, which means there is a very good chance he could find out that I'm the main story if he just looked up and made eye contact with me. But then I hear a bus approaching and, when I see that it's headed for the city, I relax slightly. All these people must be on their way to work, commuters going about their business, so all I need to do is try and look like I'm doing the same and I'll be fine. If anyone sees the uniform, they'll assume I'm going to the hospital. But where am I really going?

I don't know, but as the sirens get louder in the distance, I have to be anywhere but here.

The bus comes to a stop and everyone pushes on, eager to find a vacant seat. I'm not bothered about that, but I have to look like I belong, so I copy what everyone else is doing and, once I'm in, I find a seat and sit in it, trying to make myself seem as small and unnoticeable as possible. I haven't paid a fare, not tapping my travel card on the meter like everybody else who boarded, but only because I don't have one. I'll just have to hope no one checks for a ticket.

As the bus heads for the city, I hear a couple of young women talking behind me and, while I have enough to occupy my mind without eavesdropping on a stranger's conversation, I cannot help but overhear them when it sounds like they're talking about me.

'She's a nurse. Ask her if she's got any advice for us.'

'What? How do you know?'

'She's wearing a uniform under her coat.'

'So? It could be a costume?'

'On a weekday morning?'

'I don't know. Maybe. Besides, what would we ask her?'

'I don't know. How to pass our exams, maybe? She could help us answer some of these questions we're supposed to be studying.'

I figure the two women are student nurses, training to one day be as qualified as I am, although they'll surely dream of a far more drama-free career than I've had. I'm praying they don't tap me on the shoulder and ask me anything. It's not that I'm afraid I won't be able to help them. I'm afraid they'd recognise me and cause a scene on this bus. One student's unwillingness to bother me has overridden the other's idea to chat with me, and they go back to talking about whatever it was they were before I boarded. That's when I hear a name I recognise.

'Professor Wright is going to kill me if I don't start doing better in his classes. He's already given me two warnings.'

Professor Wright. Why does that name sound familiar?

'Not if you tell him the reason you're struggling to concentrate is because of how dreamy his eyes are,' replies the other student, as I keep trying to figure out if and how I know who they're talking about.

'Urgh, seriously? He's like sixty.'

'So? He's handsome. More handsome than the guys our age.'

'Really? You like our professor? That's such a cliché.'

'And you wanting to become a nurse just because your mother was one isn't a cliché?'

As the two students continue to talk and tease one another, I suddenly have a memory of being in a room and there's a name on a placard on the desk. *Professor Wright.* I'm nervous, I'm young. Early twenties. Unsure about something. Maybe everything. But he's there and he's trying his best to put me at ease.

'I can help you, Darcy,' he says, kindness all over his face – the student behind me on this bus is right. The professor is handsome. He certainly was back when I knew him anyway.

'I just feel so much pressure,' I go on, talking to him with apparent ease and confidence. 'I really struggled to get my nursing degree in Michigan, and now I'm here trying to get more qualifications, but is this what I'm really meant to do? My father is one of the most renowned doctors in Chicago and my mother was such a great nurse. Even my little sister is talking about going into nursing too when she's old enough. Medicine is my family's calling, but am I good enough to do it as well as them? I just don't want to let anybody down.'

'Not wanting to disappoint your loved ones is perfectly understandable,' Professor Wright says as he comes a little closer to me. The leatherbound medical books on the shelf behind him in this office fall out of view as his body obscures them. 'But it's yourself that you shouldn't want to disappoint the most. Trust me, you don't want any regrets.'

He gets a little closer now. Do I mind? I'm still nervous. He seems so kind. So genuine. Like I can trust him to give me the help that I need.

The flashback ends there, but that's not where my thoughts about the professor end. I have nobody else to turn to in this city, not when I can't find my family. What if he can help me? He's obviously still working if these students behind me are talking about him. All I need to do to find him is follow them to their class this morning. Then, if the professor remembers me, maybe he can help me again.

It has to be worth a shot.

I have nothing else.

It's either I try this or I get off the bus downtown and wander the streets until the inevitable happens and somebody catches me.

I stay on the bus as long as the students behind me do, either keeping my head down or occasionally glancing at the city that passes by on the other side of the window. It's a busy morning, Chicago is really coming alive, and for a few positive seconds I tell myself there is so much going on here that I can continue to get around unnoticed, as if everyone else has better things to be doing with their time than looking for me. But I only have to catch a glimpse of a police car to remind myself that's not true, as well as hear a few more snippets of the conversation of the students behind me.

'Do you think she's giving nurses a bad name?'

'Who?'

'Nurse Miller. The killer nurse.'

'I don't know. She's kind of infamous. Maybe it's making our job cool again.'

'The only thing that would make nursing cool again is better pay.'

'Maybe that's why she went on her rampage. She'd had enough of working hard for low pay.'

'I hope she's alive when they find her. I want to hear her story.'

'It depends if she gives herself up easily. If she keeps running, she'll end up dead eventually.'

I swallow hard as these two members of the public openly and casually discuss the fact that I might end up getting killed by the police during my potential arrest. I guess it's no big deal for them to speculate as it's not their life, but for me what happens next is absolutely everything.

As the bus empties out, there aren't many passengers left, and when we pass a sign for Chicago Medical College I realise we are almost there. The closer we get, the more students I see walking in the same direction as this bus, all of them so much younger than me, walking with far more energy, most of them laughing and smiling as if they don't have a care in the world. Maybe there's an exam on the horizon or some coursework that needs completing, but for the most part they are relaxed because they have something I no longer possess.

The prospect of a bright future.

I'm envious of each and every one of them, especially as I get a memory of being here before, making my way to the large building up ahead with a backpack on my shoulders and a heart full of optimism about my life ahead. I couldn't have known all that would happen in my future, just like none of these people can know what their future holds either, but surely none of these future medical professionals will become embroiled in the things I have.

The bus comes to a stop and the two students behind me make a move, so I allow them to pass before I get up and follow them off the bus. They quickly join the crowd, but I make sure to keep my eyes on them so I can follow them to their lecture, aware that's my quickest way of finding out where Professor Wright is.

The sense of déjà vu is strong as I walk towards the building emblazoned with the college's insignia, but I don't get time to appreciate being back in what feels like familiar surroundings, as I'm too conscious that I could be recognised at any point. I turn up the collar of my coat as well as pull my baseball cap down tighter and bow my head as often as I can, although that leads me to accidentally bump into somebody and there is a second of panic when I fear they're going to look right at me. Fortunately, they hurry on their way, not even looking at my face, presumably late for their class and with no time to spare.

I continue to tail the two young women as they go inside, and as we move down busy corridors, the walls plastered with student notices and motivational phrases meant to inspire the next generation, I really remember being here. But it's not a good feeling. The deeper I go into this place, the worse I start to feel. By the time I see the two women enter a lecture hall, I am starting to worry that I shouldn't have come this far at all.

Should I turn back?

As several students around me push to get into the hall before the lecture begins, I find myself almost swept along by their momentum and, before I know it, I am at the back of a large theatre, looking down at all the seats that form a semicircle around the lectern where the professor will soon take his place.

The doors close behind me and everybody's loud chatter becomes hushed. He's here. Professor Wright strides out of a side door and takes his place behind the lectern at the front where every medical student can see him.

He seems to command respect effortlessly and I don't think it's just because he is handsome or confident. I think it's because these students know something I seem to remember too.

This man is friendly.

But, if so, why do I feel so uneasy all of a sudden in his presence?

As I take a seat on the back row and pray that the professor won't notice me all the way up here, I get the feeling that the reason I'm uncomfortable now is because I did something to get on this professor's wrong side once.

But what was it?

And, unlike me, will he be able to remember it?

TWELVE

PIPPA

'In there!' I say, instructing the stranger carrying my injured son to head towards our cabin. As Campbell continues to moan, and I continue to doubt the character of the man holding him, I have no choice but to go along with this until my child is in a safe place and I can assess his injuries properly.

I'm praying the cut isn't actually as deep as it looks, but for now I just need to get him laid down in a comfortable bed and I couldn't manage that alone. I was lost in the woods and would still be in there now, wandering around, if I hadn't had the help of the man with me. If he does recognise us from the news then he hasn't said anything yet, or shown any signs that he's nervous around me. If he is the one who hurt Campbell in the first place before I found him, though, then he isn't giving away any clues there either.

I push the cabin door open then hold it to make sure it doesn't swing shut as the man carries Campbell inside, and I tell him which bed to take him to. As we hurry through the cabin, there is no sign of my family members. They must all still be out there in the woods, each looking for Campbell in their own chosen direction. I was the first to find him and now I wish they were all back here so they could help me with what happens next. As it is, my son and I are still alone with this total stranger.

As my son is carried into the bedroom, I find the small medi-kit I brought here for minor emergencies, and I'm glad I have it now as I guess I'm just about to use most of the basic medical items that are inside it. I also grab a towel and lay it down on the bed so Campbell won't get blood on the sheet before he's placed onto it.

'Gently!' I cry as the man starts to lower him down.

'Ouch!' Campbell groans, still clearly in a lot of pain, but I'm hoping it's mostly just his initial shock about being hurt rather than any genuine problem that isn't going to heal up with a little bit of rest and TLC.

'Give me some space,' I instruct the man, and he quickly steps back to allow me to get to my son's bedside and begin giving the care he needs.

It's hard because he's my son, but I have to go into nurse mode and treat Campbell as if he is just one of the many patients I would see at the hospital on a daily basis. That means I have to put emotion to the side, although that's easier said than done, and that's before the unusual circumstances of this are taken into account. Regardless of who I'm caring for, we're not in a hospital and I'm not accompanied by a trained and trusted colleague.

I'm about as far out of my comfort zone as I could be.

But I still have to make it work.

'Okay, Campbell. I need you to be a big brave boy now and answer all my questions,' I say to my son. 'Can you do that?'

Campbell sniffles but nods, falling into the trap that most young children do, in that they want to appear older and braver than they actually are around adults.

'What did you cut yourself on?' I ask.

'A stupid branch,' Campbell laments mournfully. 'It scratched me.'

I tenderly touch around the spot that is causing my son the most pain, and he winces, but I need to examine the wound to make sure it came from a branch like he says and not from the hands of the man who carried him here.

'Okay, good boy. Now I need you to be strong for a little longer. I'm just going to take a closer look.'

'No,' Campbell says, clearly afraid of the pain that such a thing might cause him.

'Don't worry, I'll stop as soon as it hurts.'

Campbell whimpers again but he is being very good, my brave little boy.

I examine the cut closely and though there is a fair amount of blood, I'm hoping a lot of it is superficial. I unzip the medi-kit and take out the sanitising wipes before beginning to clean the area around the wound. Predictably, the alcohol in the disinfecting wipes causes my son some pain.

'Ow!' he cries as he wriggles.

'Almost done,' I say as I focus on the wound and, as it becomes cleaner, I am relieved to not see too much dirt in and around it. I pour water from the bottle by my son's bed on it to make sure, and Campbell cries out again, but it has to be done.

'You're doing really well,' I say to my son before I take another look and, when I do, I see that the cut is unfortunately a little deeper than I initially thought. It might heal with rest and little movement, but I am afraid there is still a chance of infection and that is a big, big problem. To prevent the wound from getting infected, I need to use stronger creams; and if there is any infection already, he might need oral antibiotics. There's nothing like either of those in the basic medi-kit. I don't know what could have been on that branch and what germs might have entered my son's bloodstream. If he and the area around the wound gets worse, it will be a strong sign that there is an infection and then he'll definitely need drugs.

The kind that can only be obtained from a prescribing medical professional.

'Am I going to be okay?' Campbell asks me, afraid, and he's not the only one, though the role of a good nurse is not to show any fear.

'Of course you are,' I say confidently, putting my son's mental health ahead of my own. 'Do you think you're okay to take a shower? It will be good to wash that cut as soon as possible.'

'It hurts,' Campbell moans again, so I decide to give my boy a few minutes to rest on the bed before I force him up again. That's when I remember the man standing by the doorway, watching on.

'Can you just give me a minute?' I ask him. The man steps out of the room, meaning I can talk to Campbell in private for the first time since he got hurt.

'What happened? You can tell me. Did that man out there hurt you?' I whisper to Campbell, fearful of the answer. But Campbell shakes his head.

'No. I was playing and then I cut myself.'

'Was he chasing you?'

'No. He helped me.'

Campbell seems to be vouching for this guy, but can I trust the words of a potentially frightened four-year-old? Or did that man out there tell Campbell what to say and my son is too scared to tell me the truth?

'Are you absolutely sure?' I whisper again. 'You're not going to get in any trouble from me, but I just need to know if I can trust that man.'

Campbell looks at me, and I wonder if he's finally going to reveal that the man is dangerous and we're already screwed because he's in the cabin with us and no one else is around to help. But that's not what happens.

'He's nice,' Campbell says. 'He helped me.'

I guess I have to take my son's word for it, and it is a relief to not feel like we're still in danger. Although I'll continue to be wary of the man and not just because he could recognise us.

What's his reason for being here? What's he hiding from?

Is he even more dangerous than the police say we are?

'I want Daddy,' Campbell whines. 'Where is he? And where's Granny and Grandpa?'

Those are good questions and I can't answer them, as I don't know myself. But I can go and look.

'I'll go and see if they've come back to the cabin. Can you be brave and stay here until I get back? I won't be long, and I'll just be on the other side of that door.'

Campbell nods, clearly having lost whatever mischief possessed him to sneak out of this bedroom in the first place, but then an injury tends to do that.

I kiss my son's forehead before leaving the room, and I'm hoping that the rest of my family might be back already. But the only person I see in the living area of the cabin is the man who helped carry Campbell back here. He is standing awkwardly over by the fireplace, as if he knows he doesn't belong here but has figured he should stick around until we have had a proper chance to debrief.

'You're good at that,' the man says quietly as he sees me enter. 'Caring for him, I mean.'

I wonder what he means by his comment. Does he genuinely think I possess a natural talent for caregiving, and, if so, does that mean he really doesn't know that I'm one of the nurses wanted on the news? Or is he saying it in a knowing way, like he is well aware of my professional background and is almost teasing me?

'Tell me exactly what happened,' I say, keeping my distance

from him, as I want to know if his version of events matches my son's.

'I spotted him out in the woods. He was running around. I figured there must be an adult nearby but couldn't see one and then he saw me. I smiled at him but I guess he wasn't expecting to see me, so he got spooked and went to run away. He scraped his leg and fell over. That's when I tried to come to his aid.'

That story does match what Campbell said, but I'm still on my guard.

'What were you doing out there?' I ask before getting to the real question that shows my nervousness around this guy. 'What are you doing out *here*?'

'I could ask you the same thing,' the man replies calmly. 'What brings you and your family here? You do know these cabins are supposed to be unoccupied, right?'

'I asked you first,' I say, trying to stand my ground and hoping that it will work.

'I suppose you did,' the man accepts. He takes a seat on one of the sofas, making himself comfortable, which is a strange thing to do when this is surely an uncomfortable conversation to be having.

I glance back at the bedroom where Campbell lies but his door is still closed. Then I look to the windows to see if my husband or parents are coming back, but there's no sign of them.

'My wife and I, or should I say, my ex-wife, separated last year,' the man says, totally catching me off-guard. 'I don't know if you've ever been through a divorce, but it was an awful, painstaking process.'

I have not been through a divorce, though lately, due to my marital problems, I've certainly thought about what it would be like.

'After we separated, I needed to make some other changes in my life too, so I left town, hoping for a fresh start. I found myself drawn to nature and started coming out here, seeking the wilderness on my weekends. That's when I came across these cabins and, dreading going back to more built-up areas, I realised I could live here. I have plenty of savings from my half of the house sale, and it's not as if it's expensive to live here. Plus I know how to hunt so I never have to worry about food, and there's a stream half a mile from here that provides all the fresh water I need.'

The man does seem very believable, but do I buy it?

'I'm Hector,' he says, offering me a smile. 'And you are?'

I can't give him my real name, can I? Has he even given me his or was that a lie?

Before I can say anything, I hear voices outside and I turn to the door to see Karl walking in, closely followed by my parents.

'There you are! We've been looking everywhere for you!' Dad cries.

'Did you find Campbell?' Mom asks, looking frantic, and I nod before all three of them look away from me and notice the person who shouldn't be here.

'Who are you?'

My husband's question is directed at the man sitting on the sofa, although he quickly gets up.

'This is Hector,' I explain. 'He found Campbell out in the woods and helped me bring him back here. He's hurt, but he's okay.'

'He's hurt? What the hell happened?' Karl cries, still looking at the stranger.

'I better go,' Hector says. I agree that now is the time for him to leave, but Karl stands in the doorway, blocking his route out.

'What is going on here?' Karl demands to know.

'Karl, just let him leave. Like I said, he helped Campbell.'

I guess I'm trusting this stranger, so my husband eventually steps aside, allowing Hector to get out of the cabin.

I figure I'll get the opportunity to talk to that man again at some point in the near future, as he's staying in one of the cabins nearby. For now, I need to explain to my family what has happened with Campbell. Then I need to go and assess his injury again. There is still the nagging fear in my mind that he's going to need proper medical treatment.

If so, where is the nearest hospital?

And how can I go there without being arrested?

THIRTEEN

DARCY

The lecture hall is quiet, barring two things. One, the voice of the professor at the front as he talks through a slideshow about blood infections and how to treat them. And two, the scribbling of all the pens on notepads as the students around me jot down the information and wisdom that is being passed on to them for their future careers.

I'm not writing anything down though, not because I'm already a fully qualified nurse and should know this stuff already, but because I shouldn't be here. I'm out of place in this lecture hall, not a student, and certainly not someone who should be visible in a public place. But here I am, and all because I remember this professor and want to see if he can help me. Before I can figure that out, I need him to finish his lecture.

'Who can tell me what drug could be used to induce a coma?' he asks his audience, and two hands quickly shoot up, each from a couple of eager future nurses keen to show off their expanding expertise. One hand is that of a male, sitting down on the second row, looking very studious in a buttoned-up shirt, while the other belongs to a pretty blonde student sitting in the middle of the seats, looking less studious but clearly far more eye-catching to the professor, because he picks her to answer.

'Pentobarbital,' she says, and Professor Wright smiles and nods.

'That's correct,' he tells her, and I notice the eye contact lingers slightly between the pair of them before he moves on to the next slide.

As I listen to Professor Wright conducting his lecture with such apparent ease, I think about how it must be second nature to him if he's been doing this same thing for so long. If he was my professor, and I have a feeling he was, then that is a long time for him to have been here, in this hall, giving new students the same old lessons. Has he not got bored of doing this by now? Maybe he just loves to pass on his knowledge and feels good about knowing he's training the next generation of medical professionals who will serve Americans with distinction. Or perhaps he just loves the fact that he gets so much attention from pretty young students less than half his age.

I notice a trend developing as the lecture goes on. The professor asks a question, several hands go up in the air, yet every time he only seems to select the most attractive female students to answer. It's as if the guys in the room don't exist, even though males make up at least a quarter of the audience in here. As for the students who aren't traditionally attractive, the professor barely glances their way, reserving all his attention for the students in the low-cut tops or those with the flashiest smiles.

As the lecture draws to a close, I presume I haven't been noticed by the man giving it, possibly because I'm all the way up here at the back in a shadowy corner with my cap pulled down, and not because he doesn't deem me pretty enough. I also haven't raised my hand once, nor done anything else to draw attention to myself, so I haven't given him a reason to look my way. I'd prefer he only sees me when I approach him at the end when everybody else has gone. That'll be the best way to figure out if he does remember me like I remember him.

'You're all incredibly smart people who already have your nursing degrees from universities around America,' he says, trying to end his lecture on an uplifting note. 'You're here now to add the extra knowledge that will separate you from all the other nurses out there who are competing with you for the same jobs. So back yourselves. Know that you deserve it and know that, when you leave here, you will be way ahead of your competition.'

That seems to work in lifting the mood in here, which had got a little heavy due to all the medical jargon that has been thrown around over the past sixty minutes.

'Any more questions on what you've learned today?' Professor Wright asks, preparing to finish if there are none, but before he can, a hand goes up, and I notice it belongs to one of the students who was sitting behind me on the bus.

'It's not about today's lecture, but I was wondering what you think about what's in the news?'

'I'm afraid you'll have to be more specific. There is an awful lot in the news, so unless you want me to start guessing, you're going to have to give me a hint.'

The professor smiles wryly, and a few students chuckle.

'Nurse Miller,' the student goes on, providing the specificity that the professor sought. 'I heard she was an ex-student here. Did you ever teach her?'

My heart starts thumping faster, as now I'm the subject of this lecture and all these students with their pens still poised are about to hear about me. Or so I think, until the professor speaks again.

'I believe she was a student here, many, many years ago, but I don't recall her myself. I teach a lot of students, but I don't think I taught her personally, which I hope is obvious. If she had been one of my students, I certainly wouldn't have taught her to go around giving all the rest of you nurses a bad name.'

There's laughter in the room as everyone enjoys the professor's joke. Everyone, that is, except me. He just made a joke at my expense, but I know he didn't really mean it. Not the joke part but the part where he said he didn't know me. I'm sure I recall him being my professor when I was a student here. Why else would his name have rung a bell with me? But he seems to have no recollection of me.

Is he telling the truth?

As the students stand and begin to head for the doors, I decide it's time to find out.

I stay in my seat and keep my head down as everybody around me leaves until it's just me and the professor down at the front. He's busy tidying up his notebooks and he hasn't even noticed me yet. He still doesn't notice me when I make my way down the steps towards him, and his head is down over his desk as I approach, although he does detect that somebody is still here.

'Is this the part where you ask me to explain things again because you were asleep the first time I taught it?' Professor Wright jests, clearly thinking I'm some silly student who wasn't listening during the lecture. But then he finally looks up and, when he sees me, there are no more jokes to be made.

The expression on his face tells me all I need to know.

He definitely recognises me.

But is it from the recent news bulletins?

Or is it from the past?

'You taught me, didn't you?' I say as the professor doesn't move a muscle. 'I'm one of your old students. I remember now. I remember being here. I remember you.'

'What do you want?' Professor Wright asks, and I notice him looking past me to where the nearest door is.

'I need help,' I admit honestly. 'I have nobody here in Chicago who can help me. But I was hoping you can.'

'Me?'

'I need a friend,' I admit then hopelessly. 'Please, everyone out there is looking for me and I have nowhere else to go. I'm just trying to remember things. About my past. About who I really am. Do you remember me? I mean from when I was a student here.'

The professor takes his time before he nods slowly.

'That's why I'm here,' I go on, validated. 'I've had this flash-back of me being here, on this campus, in one of the rooms somewhere, and I was...'

'You were what?'

'I was holding a pillow over somebody's face.'

The professor's eyes widen, and I'm unsure if it's because what I just said is shocking or if he remembers such an incident too.

'What was I doing? Who was I doing it to?' I ask him. 'Do you have any idea?'

The professor looks around the otherwise empty lecture hall before making a decision.

'We can't stay here. Someone might see you. Come with me.'

He picks up his notebooks and heads for the nearest door, and I follow quickly, afraid to lose him, as then I'll just be alone again on this cavernous campus and I doubt I'll be able to make it out with as much luck as I had getting in here.

We leave the lecture hall and enter a long corridor. It's pleasing to see we are still the only two people here. Everyone else must be in classes or other lecture halls now, or outside where the sun is shining. Although we're not going to any of those places. As

Professor Wright leads me to a door and then unlocks it with a key, I see where we are going.

Into his office.

No sooner have I entered and looked around than I'm struck by another flashback. I've definitely been in here before. It's familiar from the sight of the messy desk, to the smell of coffee, to the view from the window behind his desk that looks out over a large green space where several students sit and talk. It's so confusing to be getting so many memories at once, as if my brain is a computer rebooting and restarting constantly, making me unable to save my work in time or remember where I was up to last. As Professor Wright closes the door behind me, it seems he is very clear about what is going on here.

Which is why he locks the door.

'Just in case anybody tries to get in,' he says casually. 'You don't want to be seen here. I can help you, but only if we keep you out of sight.'

That makes sense, but I'm still wary as the professor walks behind his desk and pulls down the blinds, so the window is now obscured and nobody can see in. That's why I keep my eyes on the key that's been placed down on the desk.

'Thank you for not freaking out and calling the police,' I say.

'Don't get me wrong, the reward the police are offering would be nice, but I'm not that desperate for cash,' Professor Wright says, trying to lighten the mood. 'Even as a poorly paid professor.'

I look around his workspace, at all the medical notebooks, and the piles of essays to be marked, and think about the sheer volume of medical knowledge that this man must possess and try to pass on every day, and I can't help but feel like it's a lot of work for whatever he's being paid. Then again, it must be easier than nursing, or he would probably be doing that instead, and I can see how an office like this is a little more peaceful than a hospital ward, even with all the noisy students to deal with on a daily basis.

'You must be disappointed in me,' I say as Professor Wright stands awkwardly behind his desk. 'A former student of yours turns out to be the worst nurse ever and the most wanted woman in Chicago.'

'I don't believe everything I hear on the news,' the professor replies without skipping a beat. 'I understand that life isn't as simple as what some reporter tells me on TV. There's more than one side to the story. So, why don't you tell me yours.'

'I wish I could,' I admit, shaking my head. 'But it's so jumbled.'

'Your accident,' Professor Wright says, and I nod. 'Retrograde amnesia, I believe. There has been a lot said about your condition on the news since people started speculating about you and what was causing your behaviour. Only half of what these medical experts say is right. I know the truth. Your memory is not what it was, and probably will never be the same again. Therefore, you don't know who you are or who to trust.'

'I'm just trying to find my family,' I say, and the professor nods.

'You mentioned you've been getting flashbacks,' he adds. 'Tell me about those. Specifically, ones that relate to here. To me.'

He takes a seat, so I guess that's a good sign that he's getting more comfortable in my presence. If he's still nervous to be around me, he's doing a good job of disguising it.

'More and more memories have been coming back to me recently in the form of flashbacks,' I tell him.

'Some flashbacks can be false,' he cuts in, as if he can't allow a conversation about any kind of medical condition to go on too long without him interjecting with some knowledge he has on the subject.

'These flashbacks. Will they keep happening? Will I

remember everything soon? And how do I know what's real and what's not?'

'It's tricky,' the professor says, tapping his desk, and I notice the lack of a wedding band. 'You might get more or you might get the same ones over and over again. You will probably never remember everything. And because some of what you do recall may not be true, it's almost impossible to be certain about it. Your imagination can play a big part in flashbacks. Paranoia. Fear. It can be like having a dream. Sometimes a flashback is based in reality but, other times, it's not. The problem is, when you're having a dream, it all feels real.'

'So remembering suffocating somebody here? That might not be real.'

Professor Wright chuckles. 'I'm fairly certain that one is not real.'

'How can I know for sure?'

'Well, put it this way. I've worked here for a very long time, and I don't remember anything about a student suffocating somebody.'

I guess that's intended to put my mind at ease, but it doesn't; the flashback felt so real that it can't have been imagined. But Professor Wright is telling me it was, and I guess I should trust a man who knows as much as him, though surely I know myself better.

'Where are you staying?' he asks me before I can worry about that any longer.

'I don't have anywhere to go,' I reply quietly.

'What about food? Have you eaten recently?' he asks me, and I shake my head, not admitting that I've been so stressed that I've barely even had a hunger pang.

'Not for a while.'

'Wait here. I'll go and get you something from the canteen. I'll pretend it's for me.'

He heads for the door, picking up the key from his desk as he goes.

'Why are you helping me? You don't have to. You could just call the police,' I say, stating the obvious as Professor Wright unlocks the door. He pauses before opening it.

'Because I made a promise to you when you first came here,' he says, which confuses me.

'A promise?'

'Yes. I tell every student here the same thing. When you graduate and leave here, I can't help you, but while you're within these walls, I am your friend and you can count on me to do my best for you. Now that you're back within these walls again, I'd be breaking my promise if I didn't help you.'

Professor Wright smiles at me before telling me to stand back so that I won't be in view of anybody who might be passing in the corridor when he opens the door. As the door closes, I should be able to relax until he returns with my food. But when I hear the sound of the key turning in the lock, I suddenly start to panic.

He locked the door so nobody else can come along while he's away and find me, right?

Or have I just made a very big mistake?

I've trusted him, but have I been right to do that?

Or am I now trapped and totally powerless to prevent a police officer being the next person who walks through that door?

FOURTEEN

PIPPA

I tentatively peel back the gauze on my son's leg wound and instantly begin checking for any signs of infection. It's been a couple of hours since he cut his leg in the woods and I've been letting him rest since then, as well as hoping the basic medical methods I applied will be all he needs to recover. Worryingly, the skin looks very red around the wound and Campbell is starting to develop a temperature.

My worst fears might be coming true. My son needs more care than I can give him here myself.

'It's cold,' Campbell says as he tries to pull away from me and snuggle back down under his blanket, which is in direct contrast to the warmth I feel every time I touch his forehead. That's another bad sign. While his skin is burning up, he feels like it's getting chilly.

'I'm just going to change your dressing and put a new bandage on,' I say as I reopen the medi-kit that's the only thing I can use for my patient.

'No, it hurts,' Campbell says, wriggling away from me, and I can't blame him for not wanting me to keep mauling him when all he wants to do is rest.

'I promise it'll be quick,' I say to him, which is a line I've said to countless patients over the years in the hospitals where I've worked. It's often a lie as it's not always quick, but it's a white lie and I only say it to make the patient feel a little better about things. It doesn't always work though; some patients are more scared or sensitive than others, and right now my son is falling into that category.

He groans as I wash his wound again with an antiseptic wipe before beginning to wrap the bandage around the affected part of his leg. I wish he was being an easy patient, but he never has been in all the times he's been ill in the past, although these are more unusual circumstances than those. Usually, he'd be at home now, in his bedroom, surrounded by familiar comforts. I would have taken the day off work to be with him, nursing him back to health instead of nursing other people's children at the hospital. This is a very different environment. It was often difficult at home to get him feeling better again, and it might prove to be impossible here, especially when I don't have the simple fall-back option of taking him to the hospital if his condition worsens. But I can't risk his life and, if his wound is infected, which I fear it is, things could get very bad, very quickly. As his mother, I'll do whatever it takes to save him, even if it means I might get caught by the police.

'Good boy,' I say once I've finished wrapping the bandage. I snip the end off as Campbell relaxes a little again. 'Very brave.'

I decide to leave him in peace for a little while and head for the door where Karl has been watching on. His arms are folded and his face pensive, clearly as concerned about our son as I am.

'He's okay, right?' Karl whispers, and I nod, though purely for Campbell's benefit as he is watching us, before I gesture for my husband to follow me out of the room. Once he has, I close the bedroom door and begin my consultation with the patient's parent, another thing I've done countless times during my career and often the hardest part of my job. It's never easy to talk to a worried guardian, especially when you have to deliver bad news, but that's what I'm going to have to do here.

'I think his wound is infected,' I say. 'It's still a little early to know for sure, but I can't risk leaving it in case it gets worse. Not out here. I need to do something more for him.'

'Like what?'

'We have to go to a hospital.'

Karl looks worried and for two obvious reasons. One, Campbell needs more treatment. And two, trying to get it means we risk being caught by the police.

'If there's no other way,' he says and, for a second, he almost looks relieved. Then I understand why. 'I mean, this has gone on long enough. We need to go back to civilisation, get Campbell the help he needs and then explain exactly what happened and how Darcy is to blame.'

My husband thinks we're giving up? And he thinks I'm going to try and blame it all on my sister?

'That's not what's going to happen,' I tell him firmly as he frowns.

'What are you talking about? If we're going to be arrested as soon as we enter that hospital then we need to be prepared for what we're going to say.'

'Who says anything about being arrested?' I ask him, though I'm not looking for an answer. 'What if I can get Campbell the meds he needs without anybody knowing I was even there?'

I suggest such an outlandish thing with enough confidence in my voice to hopefully make my husband think that it might actually be possible. I have absolutely no idea if it is. I have no plan. I don't even know where the nearest hospital is, never mind how to navigate around it and find what I need without being recognised. But I do know that I have to try.

'You're joking, right?' Karl asks me.

I shake my head before leaving him and walking back into

the living area, where Mom and Dad are sitting nervously, anxious to know how Campbell is doing.

'He's okay,' I tell them before they can worry for another second.

'You just said he needs a hospital,' Karl says as he follows me, and my parents both go back to fretting at the sound of that.

'Yes, I did. What I meant is he is okay, for now. Although he does need meds, ones I don't have access to here. That's why I am going to go and get them for him and then I'll bring them back here and that wound on his leg will get better.'

'Will one of you talk some sense into her?' Karl begs my parents. 'She thinks she can just waltz into a hospital and steal drugs without getting caught. Even if you do, that would be another crime to add to the list of things the police want us all for. Are you insane?'

'No, I'm just doing what I need to do to keep my family safe,' I say firmly, and with some degree of annoyance that I have to spell it out for my husband. Keeping my family safe is all I've been doing since this began.

Why does it feel like I'm working in the best interests of us while he's doing the opposite?

'What does Campbell need? I thought he was going to be okay,' Mom says, worrying, as I'd expect her to; and I quickly reassure her that her grandson will be fine once he has what I'm going to get him. 'Does he have an infection? Does the wound require stitches?'

'Where's the nearest pharmacy to here?' Dad asks, and I'm grateful. It's a practical question rather than an emotional one.

'I'm not sure. I was hoping you could help me figure that out. We could go together,' I say to my father. 'You drive. I'll go inside and get what we need. Everyone else stays here while we're gone.'

'How about I take a look at him first?' Dad suggests, the practical doctor in him thinking he can figure this out without any need for taking risks. 'We might have everything we need here.'

'No, that will only waste time. I know what the issue is and it's not going to change,' I insist, hoping my parents respect that my medical knowledge is just as strong as theirs and is not being clouded by my closeness to the patient. 'Trust me, I'd rather not have to take this risk, but we need to get going now. Karl and Mom can stay with Campbell.'

'What?' Karl cries, clearly not agreeing with any of this plan.

'You have to stay here and keep an eye on him,' I tell him. 'I know you will, Mom. You know what to look out for. Keep checking on him. Give him plenty of water and monitor his temperature. We'll be as quick as we can and, once we're back, he'll get better fast.'

'Of course,' Mom says, not needing any prompting in the nursing department after her years of experience, but it feels better to say it anyway because it makes me feel less guilt about leaving temporarily.

'Why are you talking like this is a simple thing that's going to work?' Karl says, shaking his head. 'You do know you'll be arrested at that hospital and then you too, Adrian, once they find you sitting outside in the parking lot. Then what? You lead them to us? Or we're supposed to just sit here without a car and do what? We'd be totally screwed. Campbell would get worse. I can't have that happening and us having no way of getting out of here.'

'I won't let that happen,' I say, wishing I could get on the road already because this is wasting time. I can't leave until my husband understands exactly what will happen should the worst occur and I end up in handcuffs. 'If I'm caught and arrested then I will tell the police where you are so they can come here, then Campbell will get the help he needs. I'm not stupid, I won't risk our son's life over this. But there is a chance we can get him what he needs without any of us being caught. So let me try and take it.'

Karl throws his hands up in the air, totally exasperated. I expected nothing less from him, as this is how our marriage was before things got to this point, but there's no doubt recent events have turbocharged our problems and put them under even more of a spotlight. Problems are like anything when they are magnified – they get bigger, not smaller.

'What do you think?' Mom asks my father.

'We have to try, right?' he says, looking at me. I nod.

'Yes, and we have to go now,' I say, looking back towards Campbell's bedroom, so they know the health of their grandson depends on us not wasting another second talking about it.

'We best get you a disguise,' Dad says as he springs into action, and he quickly begins gathering up anything I could use to conceal my appearance, including his baseball cap and Mom's jacket. 'I could get one too and come inside with you. We'll find what we need quicker if there's two of us looking.'

'No, I'll go in on my own. Otherwise, the chance of one of us being seen is doubled.'

I'm more than ready to make a move, but my husband is still not happy.

'I don't believe this,' Karl mutters as I prepare to leave, but he's not stopping us now.

As my parents hug, I think about doing the same with my husband. But I doubt he would be receptive to that so I just leave it, choosing instead to see my son one more time. I have no idea how this is going to end and I want to make sure that we've been close one last time just in case.

When I reach his bedside, I see that he is still restless, and his forehead is still hot to the touch. He's weary. He's also not getting better.

So I kiss him on the cheek and then go.

Next stop, *hospital*.

FIFTEEN

DARCY

I try the door handle again but get the same result. I'm still locked in the office of my former professor, in the middle of my former medical college, which is crawling with student nurses, and I can't get away, even if I want to.

And I really, really want to.

I came here because I recognised the professor's name and thought he might be able to help me, but something feels off about him. Now that I'm stuck in his office, it feels like it's too late to follow my instinct and retreat. He told me he's gone to get me some food, but has he really? Why would he help me? He said it was because he knew me, and he promises all his students that he will look after them while they're here, but that doesn't mean it's true. Plus, there's the fact that I'm no ordinary student of his.

I'm not just any nurse he trained.

I'm the killer nurse that's all over the news.

As the sense of unease grows in the pit of my stomach, I leave the door and head for the window, determined to try that for a possible escape route. Professor Wright closed the blinds, but I open them again, allowing natural light to flood the gloomy office. As the multitude of medical textbooks in this messy room are brightened by the extra light getting in, I look out and count six students sitting on the grass, enjoying a break between lectures. None of them is looking in my direction, although they might do if they glance this way and see me climbing out of the window.

The window.

I try the handle, hoping it isn't locked. It turns and clicks. The window opens, meaning I have a way out of here. I decide that I better take it, just in case. The worst that happens if I leave is that Professor Wright was trying to help me and he'll simply feel frustrated that I left without waiting for him to return. But the worst that happens if I stay is that he comes back with a member of college security, and I will have no chance of escape then.

So I go.

Clambering through the open window, I wonder what it must look like to any student who spots me doing this. Would they know whose office I'm escaping from? Would they think it a strange thing to see? Or would they recognise me, sending a wave of panic rippling across the campus, as everyone suddenly starts running for their lives as if I am some threat to them?

I jump down from the window. As my feet hit the ground, I immediately look around to see if anybody has noticed me. But nobody has. There's no commotion, although there will be if I linger, so I start walking quickly, leaving the office behind and keeping on the outer edges of the communal space where the students lounge.

I have no idea how to get out of here, but I see a door ahead and decide to go through it. I'm now in a quiet corridor. I'm just about to move through it when I hear a familiar voice that causes me to freeze.

It's Professor Wright.

He's right around the next corner. And he's talking to somebody.

I dare not move a muscle as I listen to hear if he's getting any closer to where I am and what he's saying. But it doesn't sound like he's moving. However, it does sound like I still have a problem.

'Yes, she's here. She's in my office like I said, and she can't go anywhere because the door is locked. You're going to need to get here quickly because she is obviously dangerous, and we have a lot of students here who could be at risk.'

Who is he talking to?

And why has he just told them about me?

My instinct not to trust Professor Wright at the last minute was correct, and I clearly did the right thing breaking out of his office. He's betraying me, but I still don't know who he's talking to, so I creep towards the sound of his voice, reaching the corner in the corridor. Then I peep around it and, when I do, I see the professor is on the phone.

'She's clearly deluded and saying all sorts of nonsensical things. Although she trusts me, so I'll keep her here. But be quick. She might suddenly want to leave, and I don't know what she's capable of.'

I cannot believe what the professor is saying, but one thing I have to trust is that he is talking to the police and urging them to come and arrest me.

I could storm around this corner now and confront the professor, lambasting him for backstabbing me. But I decide not to do something as silly as that, even if there would be a split second of pleasure to be gained from him seeing that I am not in his office anymore. I need to leave, while I still have a tiny advantage, so I turn and start walking.

Right into the chest of a security guard.

As we bump back off each other, I see his uniform and his ID badge as well as the radio fastened to his belt. All he has to do to know who I am is look at my face. And he does just that. His eyebrows lift when he realises he has come face to face with the woman everyone in Chicago is looking for.

'Wait!' he calls after me as I turn and run, but I don't look back as I sprint away from him. I haven't got far before I hear him talking into his radio.

I don't hear what he says over the sound of my footsteps pounding into the floor beneath me, but I do hear what comes next.

The college alarm is activated. This place has gone into lockdown.

My sense of urgency only increases. I have literally seconds to get out of here. Before I'm trapped on campus and the police swarm all over this place. I have no idea which way to turn, which way to go, which door to try, and, despite still running, I feel like this is it.

It's over.

I'm about to face the consequences of all my actions.

As the alarm blares, deafening me and everybody else who's hearing it, because it's designed to not be ignored, I have almost made my peace with being caught. Even when I see a door open up ahead and a man in a smart blue shirt and trousers emerges, I'm not thinking about trying to evade him or do anything to keep him from me. In fact, I don't even have the energy to pretend anymore, so all I do is drop to my knees and start crying, letting this man know that I am utterly defenceless and of no threat to him at all.

'Darcy?'

I hear the man say my name, but my head is bowed and my eyes are full of tears, so I figure he knows me from the news and is simply stating my name in disbelief that I have effectively landed right in his lap.

Then he says something that cannot be so easily explained.

'Get up. Come with me. Quickly! In here!'

I look up to see him urgently gesturing for me to follow him into the room he just came out of and, while I don't yet know why, it seems like he's trying to help me.

'Come on. Move!' he says again, still eager for me to follow him, so I get back to my feet and go into the room, figuring it can't be any worse than being out there in the corridor waiting for that security guard to catch up with me.

As the man closes the door behind us, he quickly looks around before telling me why.

'We need somewhere to hide you. The cupboard!' he cries as he moves towards it and opens the doors before frantically pulling out some of the boxes full of notebooks he stores in there, presumably to make space for me to take their place.

'Why are you trying to help me?' I ask this stranger who is reacting in the totally opposite way to that security guard.

'What do you mean?' the man asks me, only pausing momentarily before going back to the task of making more space for me in the cupboard.

'I mean, why aren't you afraid of me? Everybody else is.'

The man stops again and doesn't restart this time.

'You don't remember me, do you?' he says sadly, and I have to shake my head.

The alarm continues to blare. Anyone could burst into this room at any second to look for me, but until I know I'm not walking into another trap, I need to know who this guy is.

'My name is Cody,' he says before pausing to see if that name rings a bell. But it does not, so he explains. 'We were in the same class here when we were training to be nurses. We used to sit together sometimes. We were friends.'

There's something in the way that Cody looks as he recalls our past that makes me think that we were more than friends at one point, or he always wanted us to be but it never happened. There's not enough time to get into the finer details just yet, not with this campus on lockdown and a full search about to begin, if it hasn't already.

'It's okay if you don't remember me. I heard about your accident and know about your memory loss. I'm really sorry about that,' Cody says, genuinely meaning it and, unlike Professor Wright, I'm getting good feelings from this man. 'We can't talk right now. These rooms are going to be searched, so you need to hide. I'll do my best to make sure they don't find you and then, if I can, I'll get you off the campus and somewhere safe.'

Cody signals for me to get in the cupboard now that there is enough room for me to conceal myself in there, and just before I do I have one more question.

'What if you get caught helping me? You'll be arrested too.'

'I'll take the risk,' he replies without skipping a beat. 'For a friend.'

Again, I'm not convinced that a friend is all we've been or could have been, but I'm convinced that Cody is genuine. I was from the moment he saw me in the corridor. He looked at me differently to everyone else I've seen since I got back to Chicago. He looked at me like I see myself, which is as a person who made some bad choices but is inherently good.

That's why he's helping me.

He knows the real me.

Now all I have to hope is that I can stay hidden long enough to show the rest of the world the real me too.

SIXTEEN

PIPPA

Sunset Memorial Hospital.

That's the place I plan to steal from.

It's not the nearest location – there are a couple of pharmacies closer – but the problem with them is they are smaller and impossible to navigate without dealing with the pharmacist behind the counter. A hospital pharmacy is better. It's bigger, and though it means more people, it also means less chance of standing out in the crowd. I also know my way around hospitals. Not this one specifically, but the layout tends to be similar in nearly all of them. Patient care is prioritised when it comes to designing hospitals and, therefore, a standardised layout is used. Each floor is mapped out so the staff working there can be as efficient as possible, which means I have a fairly solid idea of where I'll find the rooms where the medicines are kept. I just have to walk into the hospital, read a few signs and then think and act as if I'm really a nurse working there.

But of course I'm not. I'd be an intruder. A thief.

That's on top of the crimes I'm already wanted for.

No wonder Dad is nervous as he drives us closer to the hospital.

He's thinking what everybody else is back at the cabin.

This is a terrible idea.

'What if I go in?' Dad suggests again as we cruise along a quiet country road, praying any bad luck doesn't begin now by us encountering a police car and getting stopped before we even make it to the hospital.

'No. I'll be faster. No offence,' I say, but he can't argue with the fact I have youth on my side.

'But if I get caught, you still have a chance. You can take the car and try somewhere else and get back to Campbell that way. If you get caught, what are we going to do?'

'If I get caught then it's over,' I reply simply. 'Like I said, I'm not risking my son's health. If I'm arrested, I'll tell them about the cabin and that will be that. Let's try this first.'

Dad still looks unsure but continues driving us closer to town. As we start to see more cars and the first pedestrians on the sidewalk, I guess we're almost there. I decide to try the radio again, having already tried it a couple of times since we left the cabin only to get nothing but static. We pick up a radio station now and, as we drive through town, I'm hoping to get an update on my sister in Chicago.

Unfortunately, there's nothing but country music, and despite trying a few other channels, I can't find any news bulletins. I'll just have to hope Darcy is still free and okay. If I can get my son what he needs from the hospital, I'll be able to go and look for my sibling then. But first things first. As Dad follows a sign directing us to the hospital, the butterflies in my stomach start flapping harder. It's almost time for me to put my plan into action.

As we arrive at the hospital, I'm both relieved and over-whelmed to see how big it is. On one hand, the bigger the better, because more rooms means more places for me to hide and more doors means more possible escape routes. On the other hand, the bigger the hospital, the more time it will take me

to find what I need. Although I only have to think of my son
lying in bed back at the cabin, his temperature rising and that
wound on his leg getting worse, and that's all I need to keep
myself moving forward.

Our car stops once Dad finds a parking space as close to the
front doors as possible. The idea is that I will have less of a
distance to run should I end up being chased out of here in
several minutes' time. The thought of me sprinting back to the
car with the medicine in one hand and several security guards
in pursuit behind me is a daunting one, as is the thought of Dad
having to speed out of here and race back to the cabin before
any police cars can get on our tail. But, as I open the door to exit
Dad's car, that might very well end up being the most likely
scenario.

It's surely either that or I don't make it back out of this
hospital at all.

'Be careful,' Dad says, as if he needed to, but he must have
felt he had to offer something before I left him.

'I'll be right back,' I say, feigning confidence. 'Just keep the
engine running.'

With that, I slam the door shut and start walking towards
the hospital entrance before the nerves in my body can slow me
down and make my task even harder.

With one of Dad's baseball caps on, I'm hoping it's harder
for me to be recognised. I pass a few people on the way in, and
none of them give me a second look. As the front doors slide
open and I step inside the cool air-conditioned reception area, I
see signs with so many familiar department names.

Radiology. ICU. Obstetrics. Paediatrics. *Pharmacy.*

I follow the signs for where the meds are kept, praying that
I'll get an opportunity when I get there to steal what I need
without having to stop and speak to anybody. I pass pensive-
looking family members sitting on plastic chairs, as well as
several poorly patients being wheeled around or tentatively

taking a few steps as they have a break from being mostly bedbound. There's the familiar smell of disinfectant, as well as the recognisable pace that every member of staff here walks. They walk briskly because there is always another patient to see, another appointment to keep, another surgery to be in. That's why it's always a big red flag when you see a doctor or nurse walking slowly. It means they're most likely on their way to deliver bad news.

If the patient has a chance, haste is key. But if the chance has gone, that's when things slow down.

I'm lucky that, having worked in such a high-stress environment as a hospital, I'm not overwhelmed by the volume of people here or all the sounds of beeping machines from wards. I'm laser focused on getting where I need to be. That is the second floor, and, as I reach the elevators, I skip them in favour of taking the stairs. I don't want to get trapped in an enclosed space with other people, any of whom could recognise me if they got more than a glancing look.

I take the stairs two at a time, moving fast, aware that Dad is outside staring at the door and hoping to see me come out safe and well. As I reach the second floor, I think of Campbell one more time before I hurry on my way, and now the pharmacy is in sight.

I see two pharmacists behind the counter and beyond them are rows and rows of medicines, bottles and packages lined up on the shelves, all ready to be administered to anybody with a prescription. I don't have a prescription, which is why I don't join the line at the counter full of people waiting to get the drugs a doctor has prescribed them. Instead, I focus on the door at the side of the counter and the problem of how I need somebody to come out of it so I can go through it.

Lingering at the side of the waiting area, I make sure nobody is looking in my direction – no one is. The two staff behind the counter are busy, one of them checking prescriptions and taking payments, while the other wanders around the aisles at the back, looking for a certain bottle of medicine before they can deliver it to the patient and then go in search of the next one. It's a quiet, organised operation, but only because everybody here is doing as they're supposed to. There are no line jumpers, no one demanding to be served faster than anybody else and no issue with the pharmacists finding the medicines they need because they're experienced and know what to do.

But I'm about to introduce some chaos to this place.

As I see a third pharmacist arrive and head for the door, I prepare to follow her in, praying she won't look back over her shoulder as she enters. I watch her enter a code on the electronic keypad before the door unlocks and she pushes it open – and I'm right behind her, entering on her heels. She hurries away to the counter, and I go the opposite way, darting behind one of the shelves and making sure I'm out of view from the three pharmacists I'm now back here with.

It's like a mini labyrinth with all the different aisles full of medicines, but that will hopefully help me avoid detection. What it won't do, however, is make my task of finding what I need easy.

As I hear the pharmacists chatter and the rustling of paper bags as medicines are handed out, I look at the items on the shelf in front of me. But these are not the kind I need. I see asthma medication as well as a pile of EpiPens used to treat anaphylaxis. But no antibiotics.

Creeping quietly along the aisle, I keep searching but to no avail.

Come on, what I need will be here somewhere.

But where?

I freeze when I hear a voice right on the other side of the shelf I'm standing in front of. While whoever just spoke cannot see me, we are very close. I quicken my search but reach the end of the aisle, which means I'm going to have to brave entering another one, and who knows what could be waiting for me there? Just before I can do that, I hear the voice get closer, and then I hear something that fills me with dread.

'Two EpiPens, coming right up.'

Oh no.

The EpiPens are on this aisle.

Realising I need to find a hiding place in the next few seconds – but unable to take the risk of running blindly into the next aisle without knowing who might be lurking there – I see a row of cupboard doors below me and have an idea.

Opening one of the cupboard doors, I crouch down behind it, using it as a screen between me and the pharmacist who is about to enter this aisle. I'm out of sight, but only if the pharmacist doesn't decide to come and shut this cupboard door if she should notice it open when she grabs the EpiPens.

As I crouch in my hiding place, I hear feet scuffing across the polished floor only a few yards away from me and cannot believe how close I am to being discovered. But then the feet move away, and as I peer over the top of the cupboard door, I see that I am alone again.

Not wasting another second, I get back to my feet and peep around the next aisle, where I see a pharmacist placing a large bottle of cough syrup into a paper bag. Then she leaves, heading back to the counter, so I take her place, moving down the aisle and scouring the shelves as I go.

I see some topical antibiotics that can be applied to the skin, and this is more like it. I must be getting close, so I take a few and stuff them in my pockets because they can only help. But what I really want is oral antibiotics, as they tend to be stronger and will definitely do the job without the risk of needing something else at a later date, so I keep searching.

Then I see what I need.

Grabbing a bottle of the liquid medicine from the shelf, I double-check the label to ensure it's correct before shoving it into my coat pocket. Then I quickly find some tubes of anti-septic cream that I can also apply for good measure, before turning to get the hell out of here. But all that happens is I run straight into a startled pharmacist.

'What are you doing?' the mousey-haired woman asks me, her face as pale as her white coat as she recognises me and begins to panic.

'Wait. I can explain,' I try, but it's clear there is going to be little time for talking as the pharmacist starts to back away from me, and I fear she could call out to her colleagues at any second and then I'd be massively outnumbered.

So I make a snap decision.

I put one of my hands in my coat pocket and intimate that I have a weapon in there that I am not afraid to use.

'Don't move. I don't want to hurt you, but I will if I have to,' I say, feeling terrible that I'm having to do this, but I have no other choice.

The pharmacist freezes, her eyes on my hand in my pocket, her imagination running wild as to what I could have in there that could harm her.

A gun? A knife?

The worse she imagines, the better for me. As long as she doesn't figure out that I actually have neither of those things and I'm totally bluffing. The pharmacist seems to believe that I pose a threat to her, and why wouldn't she, based on what she's seen on the news?

'Let me leave and everything will be okay,' I say quietly. The pharmacist takes several seconds before she nods.

That's my cue to make a move, so I slowly walk past her towards the door, keeping my eyes on her for any sudden move-ments, just like she keeps her eyes on me for the same thing. But neither of us break our promise to one another and, as I reach the door, I realise I am going to make it out from behind here. However, I don't expect to get too far before the alarm sounds and, sure enough, no sooner have I made it back to the staircase than I hear an alarm blaring.

I start running, skipping steps and almost tripping before I make it back to the ground floor. As doctors, nurses and patients alike all look around in confusion at what might have caused the alarm to sound, I breeze past them all, sprinting for the exit. Once it's in sight, I'm never slowing down.

I see two security guards rushing away ahead of me, on their way to figure out what the issue is, but with no idea that the problem they're seeking is about to leave this hospital behind them.

The automatic doors slide open, allowing me to burst out into the fresh air as my eyes scan the busy entrance area for my father's car. I see an ambulance parked up outside but I race past that and there he is, my father, sitting behind the wheel of his vehicle with the engine still running.

He must be able to hear the alarm, which means he must know we don't have a second to spare. He accelerates towards me, and I dive towards the door handle, leaping into my seat and slamming the door closed again as he speeds us away.

I check the rearview mirror and see security guards heading outside and looking in our direction.

But they're too late.

Now I just have to hope I'm not too late for my son.

SEVENTEEN

DARCY

The alarm continues to blare, which means this college campus is still in lockdown and the search for me is underway. But I won't be easy to find, not in here, hidden inside this cupboard in Cody's office, crouched down in the darkness beside some medical textbooks and with the doors locked and him guarding the other side. Unless the police bring sniffer dogs. Then I'll be in trouble. But I pray that I'm long gone from here before the canines turn up.

'Can you see anything?' I ask him, knowing he can hear me in here because we've spoken a little since I got inside.

'No, but I can hear voices outside,' Cody whispers back. 'So stay quiet.'

I do as I'm told; it's not as if I have much choice. I try not to let my imagination run away with itself as I hide here and think about campus security going room to room, looking for me now that they know I am here somewhere.

And then I hear a knock on the door.

To my relief, it's just the office door and not the cupboard door, but as I hear Cody go to answer it, I know he is about to face some uncomfortable questions. And I'm about to face an uncomfortable wait to see if anybody tries opening this cupboard.

'Hey. What's going on?' Cody says to whoever is on the other side of his office door.

'We have a security alert. We believe Darcy Miller is on campus. Have you seen her?'

'The woman from the news?'

'Yes.'

Cody's playing dumb, but will it work?

'Erm, no. I mean, I heard the alarm, but had no idea what was going on.'

'So you've stayed in your office.'

'Yes. I've got a lot of work to do.'

Cody is standing firm in the face of questioning.

'You haven't seen anyone matching her description?' comes the next question, but Cody says no, and I wonder if they will leave it there.

'Can we take a quick look around?'

Oh no.

I'm so anxious that I almost flinch and disturb the pile of textbooks stacked beside me. That would be a disaster because of how much noise it would make but I just about keep myself still.

'Erm, yeah, sure,' Cody says. The anxiety in his voice is evident, though he knows that saying no would only be even more suspicious.

I hear footsteps around the office, so close to this cupboard, and I hold my breath, expecting the door to be opened at any second and the security guards who I presume are out there would drag me out.

'Like I said, I haven't seen anybody,' Cody says. 'I've just been working in here. But you think Darcy Miller is here? Are you sure? I mean, why would she come here?'

The security guards don't answer that, and I'm starting to

fear that Cody might be talking a little too much. I get even more afraid when I sense that somebody is standing right outside this cupboard.

All they have to do is ask to see inside and it is game over.

But will they?

'Okay. Stay here. If you see anything, call us,' one of the security guards says, and I realise they are leaving.

'Of course,' Cody says, the relief in his voice matching the relief in my cramped body, but I daren't move an inch until they have left.

I listen until I am sure they are gone and, as the office door closes, I hear Cody coming towards the cupboard.

'All clear,' he says before the cupboard door unlocks and opens, allowing me to climb out, which I do tentatively, as if I'm still afraid that security will return and catch me out in the open. There is no reason they should do now they have already checked this room, so I try to tell myself that I'm safe. For the time being, at least. But how am I supposed to get out of this office?

That dilemma is obviously on Cody's mind as he peers through the window blinds to look outside.

'That was only campus security but pretty soon, this place is going to be crawling with cops,' he says, and I don't need to question that. I imagine he is right, what with me being a wanted woman. I bet every police officer in Chicago will be here soon, along with all the journalists and news reporters in this city.

'It's all thanks to Professor Wright,' I tell him, shaking my head. 'He called the police. I went to him because I remembered him from my past. I thought I could trust him. But he betrayed me.'

'He did?'

I nod. 'Something's not right with him and I think it's got something to do with a flashback I had. I was here, on this campus, and I was...' I hesitate to finish my sentence because I know it's going to sound bad, but decide I have to tell Cody the truth because he's helped me this far. 'I was holding a pillow over somebody's face. I was suffocating them.'

Cody takes that about as well as I could have hoped for, in that he hasn't just run from the room to get away from me. But he does look surprised.

'You think Professor Wright has something to do with that?' he asks me.

'I don't know. Maybe. What I do know is he clearly doesn't want me here where I might remember anything else. Why is that? Is there something he's afraid I might recall? Does he want me arrested and in custody before I remember everything about my time here? It sure seems that way.'

Cody steps away from the window, looking pensive, and I feel bad for burdening this man with all my problems. I've also given him a pretty big problem of his own, yet he still seems like he would rather I was here than not.

He really must have liked me before if he's willing to accept me now.

'You're probably wondering what happened to me,' I say sadly. 'How did I go from a student nurse to the world's worst nurse?'

'I wouldn't say you're the world's worst,' Cody says with the hint of a smile. 'You're probably not going to win any awards, but you're not as bad as they say.'

'Aren't I?'

'You used to help me with my coursework,' Cody says. 'You used to give me some of the answers and edit some of my essays so that they were almost as good as yours. That's how I know you're not a bad nurse, or a bad person. You were always kind to me, so I don't see why that would have stopped when you left here.'

'The flashbacks I have. The memories. They're not all good.

And I'm remembering more now. Much more. Maybe I'll remember it all soon. I'm worried that isn't a good thing.'

Cody takes that on board, seeing how upset I am about that, before he takes my hand.

'I believe that whatever you have done, if it was bad, then you had no choice or else you wouldn't have done it,' he says.

'This memory of me suffocating somebody here. What is that?' I ask him fearfully.

Cody frowns. 'I'm not sure.'

'Did anybody die here?' I ask him. 'While we were students?'

Cody lets go of my hand and goes back to the window and he makes one more check outside before answering.

'Yes,' he says quietly, his eyes still fixed on the window.

'Who was it?' I ask, afraid that this is the missing piece of the puzzle, at least for this particular flashback, anyway.

'Her name was Taylor. She was a fellow student. She was in a lot of our classes, actually. She died in our final year.'

Oh my god. Is this it? Did I kill Taylor? Was that me?

'But she wasn't suffocated,' Cody goes on mercifully. 'She died of a drug overdose. So it wasn't her. And nobody else died while we were here, so whatever it is you think you are remembering, you didn't kill anybody here. I promise.'

Cody seems absolutely sure about that, but it's easier for him as he has the benefit of a full working memory, while mine is full of holes. Before I can ask him anymore, he makes a decision.

'We need to get you out of here before this place is totally surrounded by cops,' he says firmly. 'I can see they are letting some cars off campus. My car is parked just outside. You can hide in the trunk and I'll get you out.'

'You think that'll work? Should we not stay here?'

'No, it's too risky. The police will do a proper search when they get here and they will find you. But this is a huge campus and there are a lot of places to look, so they'll be busy for a while. We need to smuggle you out while they are distracted. The longer we leave it, the more police officers will come.'

That makes sense, though I wish there was some other way. Being smuggled out in the back of a car doesn't sound fun, though it's preferable to being taken out of here in the backseat of a police car.

'Wait here,' Cody says as he goes to the door to check if the corridor is clear outside. When it is, he beckons me to follow.

'We have to move quick. Stay with me. And if we see any police, I'll distract them so you can get away,' Cody tells me. 'If not, my car is only a few minutes away. Let's go.'

He leads me out of his office now and into the corridor, which is deserted and quiet, except for the alarm that is still sounding. I wonder when they will turn that off. Only when I'm caught? If so, I hope it keeps going for a long time yet.

'Come on,' Cody says as we press on, and while this is a very stressful situation, I feel comforted by how in charge he is.

He knows this place far better than me, so he is able to navigate it much easier, and even when we see a campus security guard up ahead looking into a room, he is able to divert us away from him so we remain unseen. Then I see a door with a window and beyond that there's a parking lot, which must be where Cody's vehicle is.

Can we make it?

'Wait,' Cody says, putting one hand up. I do as he says as he peeps through the window.

I make sure to check behind us while he's preoccupied in case anybody appears from the way we just came, but no one does, and I guess neither is anyone ahead because Cody opens the door.

'Quickly. It's the light blue car. Second on the right. Come on.'

He takes a key from his pocket and unlocks his vehicle, and the trunk instantly begins to lift up automatically.

'Get in,' he tells me, and I don't delay, hopping straight into the back before he covers me as best he can with a coat and a bag he keeps in there.

I could feel anxious about the thought of being trapped in this claustrophobic space, but it is my only way off campus and I trust that Cody can successfully manage it. That's why I say nothing as I curl up into a ball and watch him close the trunk.

Now I'm in total darkness.

And I still don't know if this is going to work.

EIGHTEEN

PIPPA

It's been a nerve-wracking drive back to the cabin, the constant checking of the rearview mirror necessary to see if any police cars are following behind us, lights flashing as they chase us all the way back to our hiding place. As Dad turns off the main road and onto the track that leads to the cabins, neither of us has seen anything to convince us that we are about to get caught.

At least not in the next few minutes, anyway.

But I still can't relax and breathe properly, the tension in my body manifesting itself by how tightly I'm gripping the medication I just stole, as well as how my heart is pounding so fast that I fear I'm a prime candidate for a panic attack.

I'm sure the reports of what, or more importantly who, the hospital pharmacist saw have made it to the police, but they haven't caught up with us yet and maybe they won't. They do know we're in the area now and it won't take long for that to make the news.

Before I can spend too much time worrying if Darcy will see any news reports about what just happened, the cabin comes into view and I prepare to tackle the next problem, which is my son's health. As Dad parks, I leap out of the vehicle, armed with what I hope will improve Campbell's condition but eager to find out sooner rather than later.

As I reach the cabin door it flies open. Karl is standing there, although not with a warm expression or welcoming gesture. He looks angry, as if I haven't just been risking everything to help our child. Although when I burst past him and enter the cabin, I quickly see why. The TV is on and, as I feared, what I did has made the news.

HOSPITAL HORROR – PHARMACIST THREATENED BY KILLER NURSE'S SISTER

That's the caption across the bottom half of the screen alongside an image of the hospital from where I have just fled. News really does travel fast, even faster than Dad drove us back here. As he enters the cabin and Mom asks if we got everything we need, all Karl wants to know is if we have been followed.

'No, we're all good,' I tell him impatiently as I rush towards Campbell's room, frustrated that my husband is not sharing in my desperation to give our son what he needs to get better. 'Mom, can you help me with this?'

'Of course,' Mom replies, quickly following behind, which I'm glad about because two nurses are always better than one.

As I enter the bedroom, I find my boy where I left him, dozing, though he stirs when he hears me approaching. I see more beads of sweat on his forehead, and he groans as he wakes, so I hurry and pull the medicine from my pocket.

'What's that?' Campbell asks me wearily as Mom sidles up alongside me.

I keep my concentration on what I'm doing, because I can't exactly go back and get more meds, not after what I went through to get this. I'm also briefly reminded of a time when I was in the early days of my nurse career, working in a hospital, when a loss of concentration caused a problem. I was preparing to inject a patient with a painkiller but I was nervy, and eager to impress my new, more experienced colleagues, I rushed what I was doing. That led to me dropping the syringe on the floor before being scolded by a doctor and being told that the whole process had to begin again for sterilisation purposes. I felt embarrassed that day, failing such a simple task like that in front of my fellow medical professionals, particularly because, even though I was qualified then, I hardly felt like a professional myself at that point. It was only a simple mistake, a silly one but not life threatening, but it's a mistake that has stuck with me throughout my career. Mainly because of what the doctor muttered to me under his breath once I'd got another syringe and finally completed the injection.

'If you can't get the simple stuff right the first time, what chance have you got with the life and death stuff?' he'd asked, which hurt me at the time and still hurts me now if I'm honest. I more than proved my worth after that unconvincing start, although I wonder what that doctor might say now when he sees me on the news. That he used to work with me? That he always knew I was trouble? That he saw something in the way I dealt with patients that hinted there might be a bigger problem one day? No, of course not, because there were no signs back then. I've never been the perfect nurse but, up until things went so crazy with Darcy, I never did anything to suggest I was capable of all this back then either.

'Okay, I need you to take this medicine and I'm going to put some cream on your cut,' I say to Campbell.

He instantly stiffens at the suggestion of ingesting something he won't like, and having his injury touched in a way he won't like either.

'It's okay, Granny is here,' Mom says as she strokes his head and tries to settle him, trying to show me that she would never allow me to do something that she wouldn't agree with.

'Come on, just let me do this and you'll start to feel better,' I tell him, meaning it but needing him to believe me. I've lost count of how many young children I've had to help before, and more than half of them try to wriggle away from me when that help arrives.

'It's okay,' I tell him, trying again, but he keeps squirming and I glance at Mom to let her know she's going to have to get a little firmer with holding him, not that she needs the hint.

'No!' he cries, not having it, but Mom holds him still while I peel back the bandage and apply the cream to his wound without stopping until the job is done.

'No!' Campbell cries, but as I told him it only takes a second, and no sooner is the wound being treated than it's covered again. I thank Mom and tell her I'll take it from here.

Now for the medicine.

'Gulp it down then have some of this,' I say, showing him the water bottle, and while Campbell shakes his head and keeps his mouth tightly clamped shut, I make it clear that I'm not going anywhere until he takes his medicine. If that means being here all night and stopping him sleeping, so be it.

Eventually, he realises he's fighting a losing battle and allows me to put the spoon in his mouth, swallowing the liquid on it before taking the water and gulping it down, though not without screwing up his face as if I have just poisoned him – as if I would ever do that.

He swallows hard and makes an 'urgh' sound immediately afterwards but, as I look into his mouth, I see the liquid is gone. I guess my son is going to be mad at me for a while for what I just made him do, but if that's the price I have to pay for keeping him well then so be it.

I'm used to being the bad guy around here.

Just like I'm currently the bad guy on the news.

I go to check on the TV after leaving my grumpy but soon-to-be-well son resting. I find my remaining family members gathered around it, watching it perversely, as if they know they shouldn't be but they simply can't resist.

'Is he okay?' Mom asks me, and I nod, annoyed that she got that question out before my husband did. Looking at Karl on the sofa, I see that he's nibbling his fingernails and jiggling his legs, a tightly wound ball of anxiety that threatens to explode at any time. He's not erupting quite yet, but he's close.

'Campbell will be fine. That's the main thing,' I say as I look at the news, making it clear that it was worth the incident at the hospital, even though we're now even more prominent in the news story.

There is already a reporter outside Sunset Memorial, speaking to the camera with that thoughtful yet personal look on their face that they perfected at journalist school.

'Pippa Simpson was here only forty minutes ago, caught stealing from the pharmacy located on the second floor of this hospital that is currently home to over five hundred patients.'

I love how they have to mention how many patients are there, as if that's how many lives were threatened by my presence among them. Of course, in reality, none of them was at risk. I would never hurt any of those people, but why let the truth get in the way of a sensationalist story?

'She only escaped after threatening a pharmacist, and efforts are now being made to find out what it was she stole, as well as where she fled to. So far, the police have been unable to locate her or the man who was driving the vehicle she left in. According to an eyewitness, that man is believed to be Adrian Miller, Pippa's father, and, of course, the father of Darcy Miller, the nurse currently being sought in Chicago.'

It's hard to envisage just how many people around America might be glued to their TVs now watching this drama unfold, but it feels like the story is getting bigger, and I guess that's why my husband is losing his mind.

'What now? What happens next?' he asks me, as if I've had

time to come up with an answer for that in among going to and from the hospital, stealing vital drugs and giving them to the child we created together.

'Just calm down. Panicking isn't useful. Not here. Not ever,' I say, and that's actually something I heard a doctor say to a nurse during one of my previous shifts. It applies here too, though it falls on deaf ears.

'This goes from bad to worse,' Karl moans. 'We should have just taken Campbell to the hospital and got him proper treatment instead of this mess. He's now an accessory to a crime for goodness' sake!'

'Don't be ridiculous, he's a four-year-old child,' I snap back, tired, on edge and now very much in the mood for an argument, because my partner obviously wants one too. He complains that I never do what he wants, but this is the time I change that.

If he wants a fight, he's got it.

'I'm sick of being the only one of the two of us who takes any action,' I go on, warming to my theme. 'You know it was the man in the other cabin who carried our son back here? Not you. Not his father. No, some stranger did more than you. How do you think that looks?'

'Campbell shouldn't have been lost in the woods to get injured in the first place!' Karl fires back. 'You shouldn't be here, I shouldn't be here, and our son certainly shouldn't. You've dragged us into this and now there's no going back.'

I could scream at my husband, really go for him. I'm sure he feels the same way, which is probably why my father quickly intervenes, coming between the pair of snarling spouses and asking for some calm.

It's enough to make me bite my tongue. I see an escape route, rushing through the door to the left and bursting out to the front of the cabin, needing the fresh air that hits my face and, more than that, needing the space and calm that comes from being away from my husband. But no sooner have I gone outside than I see the light on in the cabin in the distance.

It must be him.

The man who helped Campbell.

The man I've decided to trust.

I need a break from the people in the cabin behind me.

So I walk towards the person in the cabin ahead of me.

NINETEEN

DARCY

I can feel every bump in the road in this trunk. I can also hear the engine purring away, as well as the sound of the wheels rolling over the tarmac. But most of all, I can hear the voice that tells the driver of the car I'm in to stop.

'Pull over, sir,' the stern male voice says, and if I wasn't uncomfortable enough in this confined space, it just got a whole lot worse. Cody's car has been stopped barely a minute into him driving off, which means we must still be on campus and, therefore, surrounded by cops.

'Where are you going?' comes the first question, and I feel bad because Cody is once again forced to act as if he isn't harbouring a wanted woman.

'Home,' he says. 'I've got a lecture this afternoon and I've left my notes there. Stupid, I know. It's supposed to be the students who forget things, not the teacher, right?'

I hear Cody laugh and, while I know it's a nervous one, he actually does a very good job of making it seem casual.

'You are aware there is an incident on campus and everyone has been advised to remain where they are for their own safety?' comes the reply, which is not good.

'Oh, right. Yeah, sorry. I actually spoke to a member of campus security during their search and they said I was okay to leave. Is that okay?'

That's another lie, but will it work?

'You did?'

'Yeah,' Cody replies. 'I mean, I haven't seen anything. But is it true you think Darcy Miller is here? I mean, surely not? It must be a mistake, right?'

Cody is taking a big chance by nonchalantly mentioning me, but he's doing it because that's surely the last thing a person hiding me in the trunk of their car would do. He must be thinking it won't arouse the suspicion of this person, who I'm guessing is a police officer.

'Like I said, everyone has been told to stay where they are until the entire campus has been searched,' the obstacle standing in our way says.

'Aw, come on, man, just help me out. I really need to go and get my notes. I need them for a lecture this afternoon,' Cody pleads.

'There won't be any more lectures today. Not with all this going on. You're better just going back inside and waiting with everybody else.'

Oh no.

Cody's tactic didn't work.

What is he going to do now?

'Okay, I'll admit it. I lied just then,' he says, and I swear it's like every single muscle in my body suddenly contracts.

What the hell did he just say?

'You lied?' comes the inquisitive response, and Cody confirms it. It feels like my worst fears are coming true. Has Cody suddenly had a change of heart and realised he's never getting me out of here so he might as well give up now?

'I haven't really forgotten my notes for a lecture,' he goes on. My heart thumps so loud that I fear it's going to be audible outside this vehicle if it gets any faster. 'It's actually worse than that.'

Oh no. What's happening?

'You see, I've got a personal matter to take care of. It's quite embarrassing, actually. I'm ashamed to tell you. But I really need to go, so I have no choice.'

All I can do is listen to my heartbeat and the idling engine.

'The thing is, I've been having an affair,' Cody states surprisingly, pausing before continuing, presumably because he's making this up on the fly. 'I know, I'm stupid and dirty and I probably deserve for my girlfriend to find out. But, at the moment, she doesn't know, and she'll find out if she gets back to my apartment before I do. She's supposed to be out of town until tomorrow but she's back early. My problem is that my other girlfriend's things are lying around all over the place. If I don't get back to my apartment before my girlfriend gets there from the airport then I'm screwed. Seriously screwed. So can you help me, man to man? Please, I'm begging you. Don't let me take the hit on this one. You know how hard it is for a guy, right?'

Wow, I can't believe it. Cody has concocted a fantastical story out of nowhere in a last-ditch attempt to get this person, be they a guard or a police officer, to let him leave campus. He's done all that for me? But will it work?

There's an awfully long pause, one that I can only fill by imagining the lid of this trunk being lifted up and me being discovered in here. But then, something miraculous happens.

'Okay. Go. Be quick. And if you get stopped by anybody else, don't tell them I let you through.'

I can't believe it. Cody is being allowed to leave. His story worked. The whole man-to-man thing actually paid off. If I wasn't so desperately relieved, I'd roll my eyes at the thought of two men seemingly conspiring to keep a secretive affair hidden.

But, of course, there is no affair, just Cody saving me again, and I'll be sure to leap out of this trunk and thank him just as soon as we get somewhere safe.

There's another nervous moment when I feel the car slowing down again a minute later, but it must just have been to pull out into traffic, because now we're really motoring along, and I guess we're safely off campus. If I wasn't still so anxious, I might smile at the thought of leaving dozens of police officers and journalists to keep looking for somebody who is no longer there. Although this is no time to smile, even after a minor victory. I'm still a million miles away from any kind of win.

I'm not sure how long it takes for us to get back to Cody's place, only that it's a while, and I hit my head on the lid of the trunk twice thanks to some bumps in the road. When the lid finally opens and I see Cody ushering me out, I squint my eyes at the sudden burst of light, before climbing out and putting my feet on the concrete of what looks like an underground parking lot.

'Where are we?' I ask as I look around at dozens of other parked cars, although mercifully all of them are vacant.

'The parking lot of my apartment complex,' he tells me before locking up his vehicle and making a move to the nearest exit. 'Come on, let's not hang around here. Someone might see us. My place is just this way.'

I follow Cody out of the parking lot and up a staircase before we enter a long corridor and go up another small staircase. I guess he's wisely avoiding the elevators and, as we've come this far, it would be a shame to spoil it all now.

As we reach the third floor, Cody uses a keycard to access another corridor and then he finally comes to a stop outside a door with three numbers bolted to the front of it.

'Quickly. Inside,' he says.

I go first, pushing the door open and getting off the corridor before any of the other residents around here can leave their apartments and see me. As I glance back, I see Cody make a quick check before he follows me inside and then he locks the door. Finally, we can breathe a little easier.

For the time being, at least.

'Are you okay?' Cody asks me, which is almost laughable. I feel like I should be the one asking him that.

'Are you kidding me? How are *you* feeling? That stop you went through to get off campus? The lies you told? I don't know how you kept so calm, but thank you so much!'

I throw my arms around him, giving him the kind of hug that I would reserve only for someone who has truly earned it. He has certainly done that, and more, and I'll be eternally grateful to him for the help he has given me.

And I think by the way I'm squeezing the air out of him, he definitely knows it.

'Woah, easy there. You'll crack a rib if you're not careful,' Cody says with a laugh as I ease on his torso, realising I was probably a little overzealous, but I couldn't help it. 'Just because you're a nurse, doesn't mean you need to make me your patient.'

'Seriously, I'd be in custody right now if it wasn't for you,' I go on, stating the obvious. Cody, this saint of a man who seems to have been sent to save me, just shrugs and makes it look like it was no big deal. Then he goes and says the most mundane thing a person could say after they've just accepted a guest into their home.

'Can I get you a drink?'

Now it's my turn to laugh, all the nervous energy of the last few hours leaving my body courtesy of one innocuous question about a beverage.

'Have you got anything strong?' I ask cheekily, and Cody is more than happy to oblige, wandering off to the kitchenette area of his apartment to see what he can find.

As for me, I take a second to catch my breath. I know I just had a lucky escape, but I also know I can't stay hidden here forever. It's time to make a plan to end this, before anybody gets hurt.

I'd hate for something to happen to Cody.

More than that, I'd hate for something to happen to my family.

TWENTY

PIPPA

I'm shaking.

Is it because it's chilly out here?

Or is it fear?

I'm not sure what it is that's prevented me from knocking on the door of the other cabin. But I'm lingering in the woods, the cabin with the light on still in sight, my mind unclear on what to do next. All I know is I don't want another argument with my husband, so I won't go back to the cabin with him in it just yet.

I've relaxed a little now I know Campbell is going to be fine, the drugs I've seen work hundreds of times before are surely guaranteed to work again. If they weren't, I wouldn't be out here – I'd be by his bedside – but I'm confident he'll be okay. But, just to be sure, Mom is currently watching over him, while Dad is nearby in the cabin, and with those two medical minds on hand, the patient is well looked after. It's nice to ease that pressure of worry, even if it came at the expense of the police knowing I was at that hospital, and Karl hating me even more for dragging us out here. I can't relax when it comes to this stranger who was with Campbell when he got hurt, though. I want to talk to him, find out more about him, ensure he really isn't a threat and is just some divorcee living a quiet life in the woods like he said he was. I can't know for sure, but what I do know with absolute certainty is that he carried Campbell to safety and that counts for something.

We got interrupted the first time we spoke.

Now it's time to finish our conversation.

I stop hesitating and march up to the cabin, fully prepared to knock, although just before I do I hear something behind me.

'Pippa! Where are you?'

It's Karl. He's calling out to find me, though he hasn't spotted me over here. It won't take him long to do so if he looks in this direction, and that's when I realise that I really don't want him to see me yet. Our argument is still too raw, and I can't face having to hear him shout at me again, nor can I be bothered to talk to him if I don't have anything nice to say at present.

That's why I dart down the side of the cabin so I'll be out of view. I can still hear him calling out for me, but my back is pressed against the timber structure that separates us and I know he can't see me here.

But someone else can.

'Hello, neighbour.'

I almost jump out of my skin at the sound of the voice just above my head, and as I step away from the cabin and look up, I see Hector leaning out of a window. He's totally caught me lurking around his place. Although I quickly remind myself that this is technically not his place at all, and he doesn't really belong here anymore than I do.

'Oh, erm. Sorry,' I say, apologising for no reason, but he really did catch me off-guard. My defences quickly go back up. I still have to be wary of this man, although he doesn't seem to be very wary of me.

'No problem at all. Come in if you like. The back door's

unlocked, so your husband won't see you, if that's what you're worried about.'

Hector disappears back inside, leaving me staring up at a vacant window and feeling embarrassed that he's aware of my marital troubles. But of course he is. He must have heard Karl calling for me like I heard him, and he saw me hiding from those calls. He might even have heard the pair of us arguing not so long ago. Then there's the fact he was also in our cabin after Campbell's accident when my husband came in and started demanding to know what was going on. If he had failed to sense tension between us, he'd have to have been wearing an eye mask and ear plugs.

But now he's invited me inside.

What should I do?

I think about leaving and returning to my family, but if I do that then I won't learn any more about this man and whether or not it's really safe for us to stay here with him around. It could also be useful to learn if he has any skills that might help us in the future should we need them, like how to survive in this unusual environment. Ultimately, I make my decision after reassuring myself that, even if Hector is dangerous, he wouldn't be so stupid as to do anything like try and hurt me, not when the rest of my family members are so close and could come looking for me. Maybe he really is just who he said he was earlier, and maybe he really did just do me a favour with Campbell.

If so, I really need to make sure I thank him properly.

So I go in.

I can immediately see that this cabin has exactly the same layout as the one I'm staying in, which is unsurprising as I'm sure they were all designed to look identical. What's different is how at home Hector has made himself here. Unlike in our cabin, which is fairly sparse, barring the haphazard items we managed to bring, Hector has filled this place with all sorts of homely things. There's a red armchair, a coffee table full of hunting magazines and several black pots and pans lined up on the kitchen counter. He must have got all this stuff from somewhere because none of these items are in our cabin. I look around and I see more signs of how comfortable he's made this place for himself. I spot clothes drying on a makeshift rack, as well as what looks like a tent, although it's folded up, which makes me think he must have used it to sleep in at some point but possibly not for a while now.

But then I see something that isn't as homely.

A gun.

There's a rifle propped up against a wall underneath a jacket and beside a pair of boots. Now I've seen it, I'm instantly regretting coming in here.

Oh no. What have I walked into? What if he picks that gun up and aims it at me? What would I do? How could I escape?

'Relax, it's not loaded,' Hector says, surprising me as he walks out from one of the bedrooms. 'It will be tomorrow morning when I go out hunting for deer.'

I look away from the weapon and over at the man who's sauntering into his kitchen, and he seems totally at ease with me being here, which again makes me feel like he isn't trying to hide something. But I can't be sure, so I keep my distance, and, as I talk, keep checking that the gun stays untouched too.

'I just wanted to say thank you again,' I say. 'For earlier. With my son.'

'How's he doing?' Hector asks as he opens a cupboard and takes out a tin of peas.

How the hell did he get them?

'He's going to be okay,' I say, wondering why he has such food items so easily to hand. 'Sorry, how long did you say you'd been here again?'

'Long enough to keep these cupboards well stocked,' Hector replies as he opens the tin. 'There's a supermarket about twenty miles from here that throws a lot of stuff out, so I take what I can from the trash at night. There's nothing real exciting there, as you can see with this tin of peas. Hence the gun. I prefer to eat meat cooked over an open fire, and the woods is the best place to go shopping for that.'

I look at the gun again and think how this man is far more adapted to his new environment than me and my city-dwelling family. He must be thinking the same thing, judging by what he says next.

'If you want my advice, find yourself some other place to hide,' Hector says as he finds a spoon and begins eating the cold peas, which would normally make me a little queasy, but I'm so hungry myself that I can understand why he's doing it.

'Sorry? What do you mean? We're not hiding.'

'Okay, lie to me. I don't care. It's not as if there's anybody here I can talk to about you. I'm just trying to be helpful. You and your family won't last long in these woods. Even if you don't starve, you'll get hurt. Your son has already made a head start on that.'

It could just be a genuine piece of advice, gained from experience living here himself before us.

Or that part about us getting hurt could be something more sinister.

Is he hinting at a threat if we stay living near him?

I don't know for sure, but I get the feeling that I shouldn't outstay any welcome I have here, so I try and wrap this up because, suddenly, going back to my angry husband doesn't seem quite as bad as hanging around with this mysterious man.

'Like I said. Thank you for helping my son. We'll stay out of your way while we're here and I'm sure you'll stay out of ours.'

I think that sounds fair enough, and clearly establishes a boundary between us. I turn for the door just as Hector chuckles.

'What's funny?' I ask him, my sense of unease only growing.

'Oh, nothing. Nothing at all. I'm sure you guys will have a

good time here. But if you think we're going to be able to avoid each other then I'm afraid it's unlikely.'

I'm not sure what I'm supposed to take from that comment, but I try and assume he simply means that our cabins are close and we'll probably see one another in passing without being able to help it. That's why I just smile and carry on to the door, passing the rifle as I go. I also pass a side table beside a coat stand and, when I do, I see an A4 piece of paper lying on the top of it. I then see a name on the paper, which appears to be some kind of letter. The name at the top doesn't mean much to me. But it does strike me as odd, because it's not the name I was given by the man standing behind me.

By the looks of it, this letter belongs to somebody called *Travis Goddard*.

So is that a different person to Hector?

Or has the man with the rifle given me a false name?

If so, maybe we're better off getting out of here sooner rather than later after all.

TWENTY-ONE

DARCY

'Are you sure you should be watching this?'

Cody's question is an innocent one, but he's not going to like my answer.

'Yes. How else am I supposed to know what's going on?' I reply, my eyes glued to the TV in his apartment, where I've been holed up since we made our escape off campus.

I've spent nearly all my time here watching the news, barring the ten minutes when I was hungrily wolfing down the ham and cheese toasties that my host made for me, or the fifteen minutes I was in the bathroom showering and trying to refresh both my body and mind. I can understand why Cody is concerned for me – it surely can't be good for my mental health to be watching so much content about myself, especially when it's all negative, but it's the only way I can assess the state of play.

Unsurprisingly, much of the news coverage is taking place around the college, where members of the media have gathered to report on the sighting of me that occurred there earlier today. There are even speculative reports that I'm still hiding somewhere on the sprawling campus, although some have started to accept there is a chance I escaped before the cordon went up and I'm back on the loose in Chicago again. Nobody is talking about the possibility of me being here, hiding at the home of a professor, although that might change if the person who allowed Cody's car to leave campus suddenly wonders if that was the only possible way I could have escaped.

'We're joined now by psychiatrist Doctor Eleanor Mason, who is here to discuss what Nurse Miller's motivations most likely are at this point. Thank you for joining us, Doctor.'

I keep watching as a demure fifty-something woman appears on screen, looking very academic and serious, as if she has just come from diagnosing a patient to appearing here, on national television, to talk about me. I guess she's an expert, or as close to one the media could find as they all desperately try and figure out what it is I might be about to do next.

'Doctor Mason, do you have any theories about why Nurse Miller would have been at the college?'

'Well, we know that she was a former student there. That's where she got one of her nursing qualifications, alongside the studying she did at the University of Michigan.'

'But why go back?'

'Well, it could be for a number of reasons. Perhaps she's looking for somebody. Or maybe she's just looking for answers. It could very well be that she's starting to remember more about her past. We know brain injuries like the type she suffered can heal, not always completely, but her memory can improve. Or it might be something else.'

'Something else? Such as?'

'She might not remember anything or anyone specifically. But if she's watching the news, the media are giving her a very full and detailed profile of the woman she used to be. That could be helping her find out where she came from and where she could go next.'

'Are you saying all this media coverage is a good thing for her?'

'What I'm saying is, she's definitely watching us, wherever she is. Just like I imagine the rest of her family are too. This constant news coverage is helping to keep that family together, because even if they don't have the means to update each other, we're providing the updates for them.'

It feels odd to see a stranger speculating about me and my motivations, but it's even odder when they're actually right. I guess this woman is an expert, so it makes sense that she would have some insight into my thinking, but she doesn't really know everything. Only I know what I might do next and, so far, I'm undecided.

The news presenter takes back control of the broadcast now, and I'm wondering what else is going to be said about me, but before I can find out Cody jumps up, startling me.

'I think we need a break,' he suddenly says, swiping the remote control from me and turning off the TV before I can listen to any more people dissecting my life.

'Hey!' I protest, but he isn't changing his mind, keeping the remote well out of my reach so I couldn't even lunge for it. Not that I will, because this is his house, so he's entitled to make the rules.

I guess there's no point in trying to learn more from the TV now, but there is still a vital source of information right here in this room I can utilise.

'Tell me more about when we were students,' I request of Cody. 'What was I like?'

Cody hesitates to reply, as if he's not sure me watching the news is so bad after all, compared to having this conversation, anyway.

'You were... lovely,' he says, taking a seat on one of the swivel chairs at his breakfast bar and looking a little awkward. 'I mean, you were really nice. Friendly. I guess that's why I started hanging out with you. I needed a friend, and I didn't have many on campus, especially when I started. But you were one.'

'Who else was there?' I ask, eager to assemble the puzzle pieces of my formative years as quickly as possible in case it leads me to a vital clue or discovery that can help me in the present.

'Erm, well, there were a few of us who used to hang out together, if that's what you mean.'

I press for names as Cody swivels slightly on his seat.

'Okay, um. There was Sarah. Derek. Milly.'

None of those names are ringing any bells, so I guess I lost touch with them a long time ago, or they never got back in touch with me after my accident.

'Jacob. Eden.'

I suddenly stir.

'Eden? As in the same Eden whose body was discovered in Lake Michigan?'

I stare at Cody as he stops swivelling, and I guess him going from fidgety to very still gives me my answer.

'I remember us being colleagues, but I didn't remember we'd met as students,' I say, and Cody nods to confirm we had.

Eden. The woman whose name pops up on the news almost as much as mine and my sister's. It's the name of the deceased nurse who used to work with me before my accident, and the same one who was in love with Laurence, the man who killed his ill wife while I stood by and watched, too gripped by fear, shock or blind love to do anything about it.

'Yeah, she was in our group,' Cody confirms.

I think about that before more questions arise.

'Why haven't you asked me about her?' I want to know. 'If we were all friends as students, and if the news is full of stories of Eden being dead and me and my family being suspects, why aren't you asking me if I did it? Why don't you want to know if I killed her?'

Cody starts swivelling slightly again.

'I don't need to know,' he says. Is it because he doesn't want to be carrying knowledge if the police question him? Or because he doesn't want to ruin whatever illusion he has of me being the friendly woman he knew when we were studying together?

'I didn't hurt her,' I say, just to make it clear. 'I don't know how she ended up in that lake, but I didn't kill her.'

While that statement should make me feel better, it doesn't. If I didn't kill her, I'm worried someone else in my family did. If that's the case, they must have been in danger themselves.

'It's okay. You don't have to explain anything to me,' Cody insists. 'I know she wasn't a good person.'

I frown.

'You know that?'

Cody hesitates, but it's too late, because he's already made his statement.

'Yeah. I never liked her. I mean, even when she hung out with us, I tolerated her, but I never warmed to her. I guess I didn't really see her like you did.'

'Like I did?'

'You worshipped her. You thought she was wonderful. She was your best friend, so of course you felt like that. I didn't see a good side of her. I could tell she was different to you. She told lies. She was fake. I was worried she'd hurt you one day. I didn't think she was as good of a friend to you as you were to her.'

It's fascinating to get this insight into my past with Eden, if a little concerning.

'Look, whatever happened with her, even if you can't remember, just know that I'm sure she had it coming. She could be manipulative. That was the only problem with hanging out with you. She was always around.'

'Yet you still hung out with me?' I ask, and Cody nods.

I look around his apartment for any signs of his life beyond his work. A photo of a partner, perhaps. A child. Even a pet.

There's nothing besides medical books and piles of essays to be marked. I guess he's single. Perhaps it's been that way for a while.

Maybe that's why he jumped at the unexpected chance to help me today. Maybe he never moved on from loving me when we were younger?

'You should get some sleep,' Cody suggests, as if reading my mind and realising how awkward things could get if we keep talking. 'You can take my bed. I'll sleep on the sofa.'

'No. I'll take the sofa.'

'It's not up for debate,' my kind friend says. 'I'll show you the room and if you need me to go out and get you anything from the supermarket, just let me know.'

Cody is being brilliant, and I can't thank him enough, though part of me also wonders if he just wants me to sleep in the bedroom rather than the lounge area so I can't stay up all night watching the news. He's probably right, it's not good for me to be glued to it, because a lot of what people are saying about me is repetitive.

I need some sleep. But I also need to think and make a plan. Do I stay here and hide, essentially trapped and worrying that eventually someone at the campus might figure out that Cody smuggled me out of there? Or do I leave here and go back outside, risking being seen, but at least being active again and trying to make things better?

I don't know. In the morning, if nobody has kicked down the door here to arrest me, I'll make a final decision on what to do next. But one thing is for sure; *the media frenzy around me and my family is only growing stronger.*

TWENTY-TWO

I returned to the cabin last night after my visit to see Hector, or possibly Travis. After making a quick check on my son, I went to bed. Karl wanted to talk, or argue, about where I had been, about why I had ignored his calls when he was looking for me, and then to go over our situation once again. I couldn't face hearing any of it. That's why I closed the door to the bedroom after telling him to stay out and, sensibly, he obeyed my order.

A domestic dispute is the last thing this cabin needs with everything else that is going on, but my husband and I are at war and it's getting worse. Campbell's condition is getting better – that's one positive as I finish checking on him after waking up on what looks to be a dry and sunny day.

I enter the living area to see that Karl slept on the sofa last night. There are signs of a makeshift bed there, though he's not in it now. I can hear someone in the bathroom, so I assume that must be him, which means I get to go another few minutes without seeing him, which is bliss. However, I do see someone else.

My mother enters the living area looking sleepy and unrefreshed from the night. Before I can say anything, she fixes me with a serious stare, and I know I'm about to get a telling off as I recognise her look from my childhood.

'You and Karl are going to go for a walk and sort out all your grievances with each other, and you're not going to come back here until you have,' Mom says firmly. 'It's not good for the two of you to be warring, with everything else going on. If this family doesn't stick together now then I don't even know what we're fighting for. So go and work it out and, when you come back, we can decide what we do next.'

'I need to check the news,' I say, looking around for the remote control, but Mom shakes her head.

'Nope. You're going for a walk and you're taking your husband with you.'

Mom has made it seem like this topic is not up for debate, and as Karl emerges from the bathroom, instantly tensing when he sees me, I realise she's right. We can't carry on like this.

At this rate, the police aren't our biggest problem.

We are.

'Pippa has just suggested a walk. I think that's a good idea, don't you, Karl?' Mom says.

'I'll stay here and watch Campbell,' my husband replies, trying to get out of it like I just did, but Mom is ready for that excuse and deftly deflects it.

'No, it's okay. I'll watch him. The two of you can go and spend some time together. Off you go now. See you later.'

Mom folds her arms and waits for us to do as she says, as if we're two naughty schoolchildren who have just been told to go and clean their bedrooms. Again, from past experience, I know she won't budge until she gets her way, so I don't even try to delay things any longer, simply putting on my shoes and grabbing my jacket while Karl sheepishly does the same. Then the pair of us step outside and, no sooner have we done that, than Mom closes the door behind us. I bet if I was to try the handle now, I would probably find that it's been locked,

ensuring we can't really come back in until peace has
returned.

I look at my husband and he glances nervously back at me,
neither one of us eager to make the first move or say the first
words until I decide to just go for it and start walking. Karl
lingers behind me slightly, though he is following tentatively.

It really is a lovely morning, and it does feel nice to be out,
although the longer the silence goes on between us, the more
the awkwardness grows, and it starts to feel like whatever is said
next is already carrying far too much weight.

'As free holidays go, I suppose this could be worse,' Karl says
with gallows humour and, as the tension eases slightly, I allow
myself a slight smile.

As icebreakers go, it's not exactly the best one, but it didn't
need to be. It's just words, but it's a start. He's trying, so I
should too.

'I know there's probably no coming back from this,' I begin
sadly. 'For us. For our marriage. Our family. Our entire lives. I
know it's likely gone way too far for that. But with that said, I
feel like we have to stick together at this point, otherwise all of
this has been for nothing.'

I look hopefully at my husband, wondering how he'll
respond. I've basically declared our relationship over and that
we might as well stick it out so this whole thing hasn't been a
waste of time, but is such a declaration too morbid to even
contemplate? *Or does he agree?*

'The thing I struggle with,' Karl responds as we keep
walking slowly into the woods, 'is how you say you've done all
of this for your family. Darcy. Your parents. Campbell. At what
point do you admit that you've taken it too far and it's your
fault? Because you do understand that it is your fault as well,
don't you? Just as much as it's your sister's at this point. Please
tell me you know that.'

Karl looks to me as we keep walking, and I guess he's

waiting for an admission of guilt, which would be the right thing to do to at least pacify him. I can't help but feel like this is unfair. He hasn't been put to the test like I have.

'This would be different if it was your family,' I say, risking another fight but unable to let it go. 'If it was your sister who was in trouble. And your parents. You'd understand how I feel then. You'd understand why I've done what I have to get to this point. You'd have done the same. Or at least I hope you would.'

'You hope I'd do all of this? Kill a woman, throw her body in the lake and become America's most wanted, while dragging my innocent child along for the ride?'

I stop walking, figuring this was a terrible idea and there's no point going any further into the woods if we're just going to argue again.

'What do you want to do, Karl? Leave us? If so, you can walk out of here and hand yourself in at the nearest police station. Tell them it's all me. Tell them how I'm such a bad person. A bad wife. Bad mother. Blame it all on me and maybe, if you're lucky, they'll let you off with just a warning. Is that what you want? Because it sure sounds like it is.'

'That's not what I want at all,' Karl cries, exasperated, as I think I notice something move behind him in the trees. 'What I'm trying to say is—'

'Wait,' I say, holding up my hand to shush my husband.

'What?'

'I thought I saw something over there,' I say, looking in the direction I swear I just saw movement a few seconds ago.

Karl turns to look too, but he can't see anything; there's nothing to see now except trees. Whatever it was has just gone or is at least hidden again. Now I have the unshakeable sense that we're being watched, and, as I look around, I wonder if it could be Travis. Has he followed us out here from his own cabin? Is he eavesdropping on our conversation? *Does he have that gun with him that I saw earlier?*

'There's nothing here,' Karl says, though no sooner has he finished his sentence than we hear a noise in the distance, in exactly the same direction I saw movement a moment ago. It's the sound of leaves being disturbed on the forest floor, as if they are being brushed aside by a pair of feet.

'There's somebody out here with us,' I say, and now Karl is less inclined to disagree.

'Your mom or dad could have followed us out?' Karl suggests rather optimistically. If it's my parents then there's nothing to worry about. But I seriously doubt that.

'No, they'll be back at the cabin watching Campbell. And they're the ones who suggested we go for a walk. They wouldn't have followed us.'

'So it's that other guy then?' Karl says, using simple powers of deduction.

'I guess so,' I reply quietly, not wanting to be overheard if that man is near. But this might be a good time to tell my husband about my visit to that other cabin.

'Yesterday, when I went out and you were trying to find me, I went to see him,' I admit as I keep scanning the trees for any sign of more movement.

'You did?'

'Yeah. I wanted to thank him again for helping me carry Campbell back to the cabin. But also to make sure there was nothing to worry about with him. I wanted to see if he really could be trusted.'

'So while I was calling out to you, you were with him?'

'Karl, that's not the point. I'm trying to tell you something and I probably should have told you it sooner, but we've been arguing, and I couldn't face it last night.'

'What?'

'He has a gun.'

'Who does?'

'The guy in the cabin. I saw it when I visited him. I mean, he says it's for hunting, and maybe it is. It made me nervous.'

Now Karl looks nervous too.

'You should have told me about this sooner. I need to know if our son is in proximity to a lethal weapon,' Karl cries, way too loud for the circumstances.

'Shh,' I try, though I fear we've definitely been overheard if we're not alone out here.

'What is it with all these damn secrets?' Karl goes on, not heeding my warning. 'Why can't you just tell me things when they happen instead of me having to prise them out of you?'

My husband has a point, but it's not the time or the place to discuss that. I feel like we need to go back to the others, and quickly.

'Come on,' I say, turning in the direction of the cabin and still very much feeling like we're being watched.

Karl doesn't need a second invitation to follow me, not wanting to linger out here by himself. As we go, I have something else to tell him.

'He's given me a fake name too,' I say quietly, bracing for my husband to get even more annoyed.

'What do you mean?'

'He told me he was called Hector but he's not. I saw a letter in his cabin, and it had a different name on it. Travis Goddard.'

Karl suddenly stops walking, as if all the power in his legs has ceased, so I have to stop too.

'What?' I ask him, wondering why he stopped dead in his tracks. That's when I notice the horrified look on his face.

'Travis Goddard?' he repeats, and I confirm that was the name I just gave him.

'What's wrong? What is it?' I ask.

Karl looks all around us but there's nothing but trees, though that doesn't seem to bring him much comfort.

'We need to get back to the cabin as quickly as possible, and then we need to get out of here,' he says, now talking very quietly after me asking him so long to do just that.

'Why?'

'Because I've heard that name before,' Karl says, even quieter than the last words he spoke.

'You have?'

He nods sullenly.

'Where did you hear it?'

'On the news.'

'What are you talking about?'

My husband looks around again, but I grab his arm and force him to look at me and answer my question. 'Karl, what do you mean you've heard that name on the news?'

He finally looks back at me.

'I've heard it in a couple of radio bulletins when I was driving to work. Months ago now, but I remember it because of the story it was connected to.'

'What story?'

'The family in Canada,' he says.

'What family?'

'The family Travis Goddard killed. Two parents and a child. Then he went on the run. I hadn't heard his name since. Until you just told me you saw it in that cabin that's right next to ours.'

I stare at my husband, wishing he hadn't just said what he did, but he's already put it out there and I can't unhear it, meaning that I now know my first instinct was right.

The man in that other cabin is dangerous.

The problem is, it might be too late to get away from him.

TWENTY-THREE

DARCY

I felt way too guilty about Cody giving up his bed for me after all he's already done, which was why I had another go at refusing to take it and insisted on sleeping on the sofa again and again. Eventually, after I had made it clear that neither of us was actually going to get any rest until he agreed, Cody went into his bedroom, but only after making me the best bed he could on the sofa.

It was sweet to watch him try to make it as comfortable as possible for me, putting down a sheet, unfurling a spare blanket and plumping up a couple of pillows, all in the hope that it would make it cosy enough to get several hours of sleep. I appreciated the effort, as I've appreciated everything else he's done since we recently reunited. As I settled down on the sofa, I told him a white lie, which was that it was very comfy and I felt tired enough to fall asleep in minutes. The truth was I was well beyond the point of sleep, and I had absolutely no intention of shutting my eyes once he left me alone. All I really wanted to do was turn the TV back on so I could watch the news and keep learning more, both about the current search for me and my family, and my history that has led me to this point.

Once Cody had retired to his bedroom and closed his door, I had quietly picked up the remote control and turned the television on, lowering the volume until it was only just audible, and then I began my news binge. Needless to say, I haven't slept a wink all night. The sun is up, but Cody isn't, so I'll keep watching until he appears.

My long night and lack of sleep has been worth it though, because I've learned a lot.

Among all the bulletins about the ongoing search, which didn't have any tangible updates or suggestions that the police had a clue where I was, I discovered a programme that was profiling me and covering the history of my life. For someone with memory loss, it was like striking gold, because I was able to sit and watch my entire life being discussed and dissected, and it allowed me to fill in several gaps in my memory, as well as refresh the things I have recently started to remember.

It began with covering my childhood. How I was born to Adrian and Scarlett Miller, and how I spent part of my childhood in a modest home in a middle-class suburb of Chicago, before we all moved to the huge house in Winnetka. That's the house that the public are now very familiar with, as it's where the police have been searching for clues, the same place I returned to earlier and almost got caught. It was surreal to see photos of my home on national television, as well as several photos of me as a child and in school uniform. I don't know who provided the media with these images, or if they were used without permission, but I saw several snaps of me and my sister together, as well as hearing discussions about where I was educated and whether anything in my childhood could have predicted what I would go on to do as an adult.

The consensus was that I had a very normal upbringing so it must have been when I moved out of home that things began to unravel. Of course, the first place I moved to after home was university in Michigan, and then after that medical college closer to home to gain further, more specific qualifications. That was when the campus I recently escaped from was mentioned, although there was nothing about Professor Wright, which is still bothering me. The timeline moved on to my nursing jobs, the hospitals I worked at in Chicago. There were photos of me in uniform, looking normal, safe, dependable, and basically like the kind of woman anybody would feel okay leaving their loved one in the care of. Tellingly, there was a comment about how I had a lack of relationships. No boyfriends to speak of. Certainly no husband. No kids. A bit of a loner.

What made me that way?

For anybody who didn't know where the story was going, they might have been forgiven for wondering why I was newsworthy, as everything about my life up to when I reached Chicago was very mundane. But then recent events came in, and suddenly it would have been strikingly obvious. The bodies in Lake Michigan – Laurence, the husband of the woman I once nursed during her ultimately doomed battle with cancer, and Eden, my colleague, and best friend. Both of them connected to me and both of them dead. Then the sightings of me in Florida, and Parker's death in hospital and my possible connection to it, especially once the CCTV footage from the hospital was checked and I was seen rushing from the building in the immediate aftermath of him dying. That CCTV footage had been shown as part of the news feature, telling me that it had made it into the public realm, and I wonder how many people have viewed it and already made their minds up about me as they watched me fleeing that hospital in my nurse's uniform.

I thought about how Cody told me he never warmed to Eden when we were students together, but there was no mention of any negative character traits on her part on the show, just how she was likely a poor, innocent victim of mine.

It's all so one-sided and biased, I kept thinking as I realised something awful.

Nobody will ever hear my side of things unless I get caught.

As the news piece concluded and my story arc of going from innocent child to villainous nurse was seemingly complete, the one thing that the producers of the programme seemed to agree on was that there was no single trigger that could have led to the events. They couldn't identify the exact tipping point when I went from being a law-abiding nurse to America's most wanted, so they assumed something caused it in adulthood. Either that, they surmised, or it was the terrible consequence of actually having too perfect a childhood, which sounded ridiculous to me.

Without knowing for sure, I keep being drawn back to the thing that's bugging me. It's the flashback I have of suffocating somebody while a student, and also the fact Professor Wright so quickly tried to get me arrested when I went to him for help.

'Please tell me you got some sleep,' Cody says, catching me as he enters the room.

'Er, yeah, I did,' I lie, grabbing the remote and turning the TV off, hoping he has no idea I've had it on for hours.

I notice Cody is wearing a suit and, as he starts to make a coffee, I guess he has a busy day planned at work.

'I've got to go into work. All campus employees have been called in for a meeting and it will seem strange if I'm not there,' Cody says as he takes out two cups, assuming I need a caffeine hit too. 'I've also never had a sick day in all the time I've worked there, so it would be suspicious if I had one the day after the police came to campus.'

I agree with that thought.

'You'd think I've changed a lot if you could remember me as a student,' Cody chuckles to himself as he makes our drinks. 'I was always skipping lectures by feigning illness. Not anymore. I guess I've finally grown up.'

I smile, though part of me wonders if the reason Cody

hasn't taken more impromptu days off from his job is because he doesn't have much to skip work for. As a student, I'm sure there were parties and friends and lovers to hang out with. But now? It doesn't seem like Cody has much going on beyond work, at least until I ran into him.

'Are you going to be okay here while I'm gone?' Cody asks me as he hands me a coffee. I stare down into the hot liquid; my thoughts are swirling just as much as the steam rising up towards me.

'I know I'm not going to be able to hide forever,' I admit. 'The police will find me eventually. But what if it's not about prolonging my freedom, but rather remembering as much as possible so I can make things right before I'm locked away.'

Cody seems surprised by my statement.

'What do you mean, *make things right?*'

I almost answer that, because I do have one specific thing in mind, but I keep it to myself at the last second. I know what he'll say if I tell him. He'll try and talk me out of it, so I stay quiet and take a sip from my coffee.

'Look, I'll be back from work around six. Until then, there's plenty of food in the fridge. Take a shower. Read a book. Try and relax. Don't watch the news. We can figure this out tonight. Okay?'

'Okay,' I say quietly, not intending to do any of that, but I need Cody to leave so I can get on with what I really want to do. Just before he goes, he disappears back into his bedroom to get something and, when he does, I notice his campus security pass hanging out of the pocket of his rucksack.

Without wasting the opportunity, I quickly take it and hide it before he returns. As he picks up his bag and says goodbye, he has no idea that I have the thing he needs to get easily around the campus. Presumably he'll notice as soon as he gets to work, and he might guess that I took it, but it'll be too late by then. I'll have what I need to get where I need to go.

I'm going back to see Professor Wright. It might seem a risky and reckless thing to do, but I need answers. This time, I'm not leaving until I find out exactly what that man might be hiding about my past. I have a feeling that whatever triggered me into eventually making some serious mistakes in my career began when I was training to be a nurse under his watch.

TWENTY-FOUR

PIPPA

If there's one thing guaranteed to get a mother running, it's finding out that her child is in close proximity to a potential serial killer.

I'm sprinting through the woods now, my husband just ahead of me because he's faster, though I'm no less determined to get to where we're going quickly. We're both racing to get back to the cabin after coming to the harrowing realisation that the mysterious man who's sharing this secluded space with us is wanted for an awful crime in Canada. According to my husband, the name I saw on that letter in the other cabin corresponds with the name of the man who's wanted across the border for multiple murders.

Travis Goddard is an extremely dangerous person.

He's a killer.

And he's living right next door to my family.

I'm desperate to get back and make sure Campbell and my parents have been okay since we left them to go for our walk, but I'm also aware I felt like we were being watched in the woods. Travis might be out here with us somewhere. That thought is all I need to put extra speed in my steps, and wherever he is I plan to keep us all moving quickly enough so he cannot catch us.

While my husband has always been against the idea of us being here, I felt it was our best option. Now I know who we have for a neighbour, I'm totally against the thought of staying here for a second longer than we need to. As soon as we get back to the cabin, we're packing up and getting the hell out of here and as far away from that man as possible.

I just hope we have enough time to do it.

It's a relief when our cabin comes into view through the trees ahead, but I won't be able to relax until I get inside and see that my loved ones are okay, so I don't slow down. Neither does Karl, who reaches the cabin first and bursts inside, temporarily leaving me out here alone, which causes me to nervously look back over my shoulder to ensure we're not being chased, if Travis was actually out in the woods with us. I can't see him, so I make it back to the cabin safely, though no less paranoid about where that man actually is.

'Slow down. You're not making any sense,' I hear my father saying to Karl as I go inside and see my family gathered in the living area. Campbell is sitting beside my mother with a cup of juice in hand, and he's looking much healthier than yesterday, though still a little pale, and clearly clingy for his grandmother.

'We need to leave, right now!' Karl cries, I'm guessing for the second time since he burst in here, such is the stressed way he gets that sentence out.

'Leave? What are you talking about?' Mom asks as she looks to me, and I can tell by her expression that she's wondering if the two of us have had another argument. For the first time in a long time, my husband and I are in agreement, so I need to make that clear as quickly as possible.

'Karl's right. We're leaving this very minute,' I say firmly. 'Quickly. We need to pack our things and get out of here. I'll explain in the car, but we need to get going as soon as possible.'

I decide to hasten this process by picking up Campbell to encourage my mother to get moving too. It also does the job of keeping my son as close to me as possible, which is what I plan to do now until we are well away from here.

'Come on. Let's get going,' I say as I carry Campbell to the bedroom to start packing, and Karl is right behind me, just as eager, though my parents are dawdling behind him. They still don't know the severity of the situation, but it'll be hard to tell them with Campbell in earshot. I don't want to risk panicking him, but I also don't want to panic my parents if I can help it, although it seems I'm going to have to as they continue to demand answers.

'Will somebody tell us what is going on?' Dad cries, and as he and Mom have stopped following, I guess they're not going to do as I say and start packing until they know.

'Here, take Campbell and I'll be right in to help you,' I say, transferring our son to my husband, and he takes him into the bedroom while I go back to have a quiet word with my parents.

'Okay, I need you to try and stay calm because we don't want Campbell to get upset,' I say in a low voice as Mom and Dad listen carefully. 'It's that man in the other cabin. We think he's wanted for murder in Canada, so we could be in danger if we stay here. That's why we need to leave. Do you understand?'

'Murder?' Mom says, a little too loudly, but before I can shush her I hear something outside the cabin.

Is Travis out there? Has he just overheard us?

I go to a window and peer outside, but I don't see anything. I could have sworn I heard something move close by.

'We need to go,' I say again for the umpteenth time and, finally, Mom and Dad know better than to delay. They go to their room to start packing, and I rush to find Karl, who is busy throwing things into a bag while Campbell whines beside him, asking where we're going now.

'We'll tell you in the car,' I say to try and appease my son, but it's never that simple with a four-year-old, and Campbell proves it by continuing to whine. Unlike most other times in our lives, however, it doesn't slow his parents down. We're doing what we need to do.

We gather up everything we own in record time, as do Mom and Dad, and while Campbell is still peppering us all with questions, I don't care as long as those questions continue in the car while we're speeding away from here. But just as I'm about to step outside with my suitcase in hand, I take another look out the window. I wish we'd skipped the packing entirely and just left already.

Travis is walking towards our cabin.

'He's coming,' I say to alert everybody else, loud enough for them to get the warning but not so loud that the man approaching might hear.

Why is he coming here?

What does he want?

Does he know we're running away from him?

'What should we do?' Mom asks me. I look at Campbell, as our decision has to be what's best for him. I cannot risk putting him in any immediate danger, so as far as I'm concerned that rules out trying to run past the killer in our midst.

'We need to stay calm,' I say. 'We can't let him know we're trying to get away from him, or that we know who he is. He might think we're going to tell the police where he is.'

Everyone agrees with my point, which is helpful because we're rapidly running out of time.

'Let me talk to him,' Dad says, starting for the door, but I stop him.

'No, I'll talk to him. He knows me best,' I say, taking responsibility. 'Take Campbell into one of the bedrooms. And hide the suitcases.'

Everyone springs into action, Mom taking Campbell out of

sight, while Dad and Karl do the same for the luggage. They manage to do this just before the knock on the door.

'Hey. Is everything okay?' I say as breezily as I can as I greet Travis, who I remind myself I need to call Hector, because he shouldn't know I'm aware of his real name.

'I was just going to ask you guys the same question,' Travis replies. I notice he's looking over my shoulder, but nothing will look out of place behind me as all the suitcases have been moved. 'I saw you and your husband running in here. It seemed like there was a bit of a panic.'

'Oh, that? It was nothing. We were just playing a game,' I say, feigning laughter.

'A game?'

'Yeah. We were racing each other back here. My husband won, unfortunately for me.'

I laugh again but it's a terribly fake one, and I fear Travis sees through it. But, if he does, he doesn't comment on it directly.

'Oh, I see. It just looked like you were stressed.'

'Stressed. No, not at all.'

I'm extremely stressed having this conversation, but I'm trying to hide it as best I can.

Travis looks past me into the cabin again.

'Where is everyone?' he asks, prying further.

'Just in their bedrooms,' I say with a shrug. 'Relaxing. Having a lie down. What are you up to?'

I hope turning the conversation back on him will stop him from noticing how uncomfortable I am in his presence.

'I was just going to go and take a walk. Any of you care to join me?'

Absolutely not.

'Oh, erm. Thanks, but like I said, everyone's quite tired, so I think we're good.'

'Even you?'

'Me? Um, yeah, I'm going to have a rest too. But thank you. You enjoy your walk.'

Travis stares at me for several long seconds before smiling and then turning away. But I feel cold, because I know that smile was as false as my laughter. I feel even worse when, after closing the door and going to the window, I watch him return to his cabin rather than head out for that walk he said he was going on.

He's onto us. He knows that we know who he is. And now he doesn't trust us.

I keep staring at his cabin, aware that he could be at one of the windows now too, watching us to see what we do next. How will it look if he sees us rushing out of here with our suitcases just after I told him we were chilling out? What if he chases after us?

That's why I decide we can't go yet.

We'll wait for darkness to fall and try and sneak away then.

We need to get out of here without him realising we're going.

But can we do it?

TWENTY-FIVE

DARCY

My return to the college campus feels even more fraught with danger than last time, given how I was spotted here yesterday and caused a huge search to commence that made the national news. If nobody was particularly looking out for me when I arrived here yesterday then they certainly will be today. That's why I've changed my appearance, having stolen a jacket from Cody's wardrobe so I'm at least wearing a different colour to the one I had on yesterday. I also found a baseball cap in his bedroom, so I've replaced that too. I still have my nurse's uniform on beneath the coat though, feeling like I don't want to leave it behind as it connects me to the woman I used to be and is safe to wear as long as it isn't visible.

I spot several police officers in the distance as I approach, walking among numerous students. Beyond them, I see several more stationed outside a large building with the word 'Cafeteria' above the door. There's a sizeable police presence here, but there's a big student population too, and I'm doing my best to make it seem like I belong in the latter, walking with my head down but with purpose rather than with timidity. One of the things that is emboldening me is that I have Cody's access pass on me.

I use it to swiftly unlock a side entrance door and enter a corridor that is mostly quiet, except for a couple of students who quickly disappear into lecture halls, most likely latecomers who don't want to annoy their lecturers any more than they already might have. I watch all the doors close until I'm totally alone, then I move down the corridor, peeping through a couple of the windows on the doors as I go, to make sure everyone around here is occupied. They certainly are, as I see lectures have commenced and dozens of faces stare straight ahead at whoever it is giving them their lesson today.

I'm close now to where I sat in on Professor Wright's lecture yesterday and that's on purpose. I want to see if he's occupied already. If so, I will know that he isn't in his office, and that will give me the chance to have a snoop around.

I recognise the lecture hall where he was working yesterday, so I cautiously peep through the window and, when I do, I see the man himself, standing confidently at the front, speaking to all his students. A slide about haemoglobins is on display behind him. I stare at him for a few seconds, recalling how he was so quick to betray me and call the police, and it only fuels my desire to know why he tricked me and wanted me out of his way as quickly as possible.

Moving on past the lecture hall, I retrace my steps from the previous day, another sign that my memory is improving constantly now, until I find myself outside Professor Wright's office. As I try the door handle, I'm hoping it isn't locked. It isn't, so I slip quickly inside and close and lock the door behind myself, before taking another look around. It's certainly easier to do that without the professor in here with me, pretending to be my friend, distracting me with false promises of help.

I work efficiently, opening desk drawers, rummaging through documents, hoping to come across something, anything, that might trigger another one of my flashbacks or give me more of an insight into the man who works here. Emboldened by the sense that I'm already running on borrowed time, and I need to try and make any past problems right before I'm arrested, I'm desperate to know if the professor is hiding something terrible about my past. But, so far, I haven't found anything damning. Not on his desk, his bookshelf or anywhere else in this office space.

Nothing is coming back to me. Not even a damn flashback. Maybe they're over. Maybe I've remembered everything I ever will, and the rest is lost to time. Then I stub my toe on the edge of the small sofa Professor Wright has in the corner of the room, and it brings tears to my eyes, as it's so painful. But, as I look around with tearstained vision, a flashback does come – of me here, in this office, crying.

Not only that.

I'm begging.

I see myself with Professor Wright, though we're both much younger and we're in the middle of a passionate debate.

'I can't do this,' I'm saying in angst. 'It's not right. I have to tell somebody what happened. It's only fair on her family.'

'Do that and I'll see to it that you are expelled from here and your academic reputation will be ruined. Your credentials will be cast into doubt and you will never become a nurse,' Professor Wright snaps back, his anger matching my level of distress.

'How can you do this to me?' I cry. 'And how could you do this to her? She's dead because of you!'

The flashback is a haunting one, and I put my hand over my mouth in shock as I recall it. Professor Wright was threatening to ruin my potential nursing career before it had even begun, and all because I knew he had taken someone's life.

She's dead because of you. Who was I talking about?

I think back to what Cody said. He told me somebody died

here. What was her name again? Taylor, was it? Is that who I was referring to when I was in here all those years ago shouting at the professor? Did he have something to do with her death? Or was it me? How does my memory of me suffocating some-body relate to it all?

I suddenly feel like I need to get out of this room, as if the walls are closing in on me and will soon be squeezing the breath out of me if I remain. I go to the door, thankful when I burst through it and don't see anybody on the other side. No student, no security guard, and best of all no professor.

I accelerate down the corridor, looking for a way out, but I soon realise I've gone the opposite way to where I came in and now I'm lost. There are so many doors, but none of them have windows so I can't even see what's on the other side. It would be incredibly risky to just choose one and go through it. But I'm still so unsettled by the flashback that I'm not thinking clearly. I blindly pick a door and, when I enter the room, I see what looks like a mock hospital ward. There's a row of beds along one wall as well as monitoring machines for things like blood pressure and heart rate sitting beside each one. It looks like this is a place nurses could practice being in a hospital, moving among patients, taking notes, conducting simple medical checks – a low-stakes environment before they're transferred to the real thing and it becomes a matter of life and death.

I move along the beds, all of which are mercifully unoccu-pied, nor is there any sign of student nurses or professors either. I have this room to myself. As I walk, I wonder if I was once here before, practising with other students, preparing for what I thought would be a long and fulfilling career in medicine. I can imagine myself being extremely conscientious, eager to learn, meticulous over the details that I was being taught, but not afraid to make a mistake, because that is always the quickest way to learn. I wonder if I was one of the top students in the class, a bright star earmarked for greatness among my peers, or if

I was somewhere in the middle, just another student passing through here, nothing special about me at all.

It's only as I reach the last bed that I remember something else – an actual, concrete memory that not only proves I've been in this room before but that I saw something truly shocking.

It's a vision of Professor Wright, forcing himself onto another woman.

She's a student and she's begging him to get off her, but he isn't stopping, and the only thing that does make him stop is when I tell him to do so.

So that's what happened. I caught him assaulting another student and, when I threatened to reveal that fact, he threatened to have me thrown out, leaving my nursing career under threat.

A sudden sound of smashing glass behind me makes me spin around. I see a woman wearing a white lab coat staring back at me in horror. It's as if every muscle in her body has frozen, and it doesn't take me long to figure out why. She recognises me and she's totally afraid.

'Please stay calm. I'm not going to hurt you,' I say, opening up my palms to show that I mean her no harm. Not that it helps relax her in any way – she remains frozen to the spot.

'I'm leaving,' I say calmly, making a slow movement for the same door through which this woman entered. 'Just stay in here and give me the chance to go. Okay?'

The woman is motionless.

'No alarms. Promise?' I try.

The woman still does nothing, but that's better than her running. I ease myself past her, wondering if she is a teacher here or perhaps an older student. Whoever she is, she is utterly terrified of me, which I use to my advantage as I am able to leave the room and get back out into the corridor, where I hasten my pace. That woman might snap out of it at any second and raise the alarm, so I need to be gone before then. I find my way back outside before rushing through the parking lot, aiming for the street beyond it. But it's as I'm moving past the rows of cars that I hear something awful.

'Darcy!'

Someone has just called my name and, as I turn around to see who it was, I'm imagining a police officer with a wide grin, thrilled that they're the lucky cop to have caught me out of all of their possible colleagues who could have taken the glory instead. But it's no police officer. It's Cody, and as he reaches me he looks seriously annoyed.

'You stole my access pass,' he says as he sees it in my hand and swipes it from my grasp.

'I'm sorry,' I say lamely, relieved I've been caught by my one friend and nobody else.

'What the hell are you thinking, coming back here again after yesterday? Are you insane? And using my pass too? The police will think I gave it to you if they catch you!'

'I'm sorry. I really am. I needed to get back inside. It's Professor Wright. I remember what he did now. He assaulted a student, and I caught him.'

'What?'

'Right here on campus. I caught him attacking her. He stopped when I saw him, although when I tried to report it, he threatened me. Do you know anything about this?'

Cody looks stunned. 'No, I've got no idea what you're talking about.'

'That student who died,' I say, trying to focus his mind.

'Taylor?'

'Yes, is there a photo of her anywhere? I want to see if it's the same woman from my flashback.'

Cody quickly takes out his phone, prompted by me reminding him that I've been spotted again here so we shouldn't hang around longer than we need to. 'There were news articles online when she died,' he says as he searches for one of them.

When he shows me his screen, it's the same woman I just saw in my flashback.

'That's her. That's who Professor Wright was attacking. Do you think he killed her to keep her quiet?'

'What? No. I told you, she died of a drug overdose. Look, it's right here. The article mentions the coroner's report. It was a definite overdose. No suspicion of foul play.'

My eyes scan the words in the news article, and Cody is right. But just because Taylor died from drugs, it doesn't mean the professor didn't cause it.

'What if she was trying to forget what he did to her?' I ask Cody fearfully. 'What if the assault scarred her? Or what if Professor Wright was putting pressure on her to stay quiet, or worse, she was afraid he was going to try again? Can't you see? He might have indirectly caused that overdose because his actions led to her taking those drugs.'

'That's a very serious accusation. And it was a very long time ago. Even if you're right, he's gotten away with it for all these years, and he's hardly likely to admit to it now, is he?'

'I don't know. If I can put him in a pressured situation, maybe I can get a confession out of him. This is why he was so desperate to have me arrested the other day before I could remember anything,' I realise now. 'I'm a threat to his secret.'

'I don't understand how this is going to help you,' Cody says.

'Because any link to my past helps me learn more about myself. Whether it triggers another flashback or just helps me fill in some blanks. But I'm not being selfish. Maybe I've been guilty of that before, so this is also about helping Taylor, or at least her parents,' I reply firmly. 'If they can find out why their daughter overdosed, it might make them understand it better. And then at least one good thing can come from me being back here.'

'So how do we do that?' Cody asks, looking around to make

sure no one else is wandering through this parking lot before he can smuggle me out of sight again.

'I need you to set up a meeting with Professor Wright,' I tell him. 'Do it tonight. He'll think it's only the two of you. Tell him it's something to do with work. I just need you to get him somewhere safe where I can confront him. Then I'll do the rest.'

'No, this has gone too far. I've already risked too much for you,' Cody says. 'I could lose everything for you, and you repay me by stealing from me?'

Cody looks like he could walk away and leave me to fend for myself, yet he isn't actually moving. He's still here, which tells me he still cares.

'Please,' I say, taking his hand. 'Just help me one more time. Then this will be over. I promise.'

I don't remember any of the lessons my parents taught me as a child, but I'm pretty sure, if I could, one of them would have been to not make promises if I don't know I can keep them. But that's just what I have done to Cody, and, as he agrees to set up the meeting with Professor Wright, I have no genuine idea if this will be over soon.

Or if it's only just beginning.

TWENTY-SIX

PIPPA

It's been an incredibly long wait for the sun to set but, now that darkness is falling, it's almost time for me and my family to sneak out of this cabin, get in our car and get away from the killer who lives so close to us. We're all packed and ready to go, as we have been for several hours, but I haven't dared try our escape in daylight. I'm well aware that Travis could see us and try and intervene if he realised we were scarpering. But as the light dims outside, it will make it harder for him to see us. Sure, he'll hear the car engine when it starts, but by then it will already be too late, because Dad can just hit the accelerator pedal and we're gone. The hard part is getting into the car in the first place, but our odds of success are increasing the darker it gets outside the windows.

'Five minutes then we'll go,' I say to my parents before going into the bedroom to check on Campbell, who is still resting in his bed with his father beside him. Ideally, I wouldn't want my son to move tonight, preferring he get a good night's sleep to ensure his recovery isn't delayed by extra fatigue. But I'm not spending another night here, not now I know the truth about the man in the next cabin, so I have no choice but to drag my poorly boy out of this warm bed and into the cold car. I'll just have to hope that it doesn't make him any worse.

'Are we all ready to go on another adventure?' I say cheerily, trying to make this as fun as possible, even though the reality of it is far from that. But while Campbell doesn't know the full extent of our problems, even he is smart enough to realise that us leaving late at night is not for adventure purposes.

'I'm tired,' he says wearily, and I know he'd rather stay in bed. I wish I could go to bed too. Once we leave here, I don't know where the next opportunity will be for us to lay our heads down on a pillow. But it's not an option and I make that clear.

'Come on, let's get going. The sooner we do, the sooner we can go to the next cool place.'

'I just want to go home,' Campbell moans. 'Is that where we're going?'

Karl and I look at each other, and I'm just about to be honest and say no, when my husband speaks first.

'Yeah, we're going home, son,' he lies. 'So come on, let's go.'

That does the trick of getting Campbell out of bed, though I'm not happy about how it was done, and I let Karl know as we leave the room.

'Why did you say that? Now he's going to get upset when we don't go home.'

'We had to get him moving,' Karl replies with a tired shake of the head. 'My way was quicker.'

I'm not starting another argument now, just as we are about to get in the car and be in extremely close proximity to each other for the next several hours. I leave it and join the rest of my family by the door, our bags packed and ready to be carried to the trunk.

'Anything on the news?' I ask Dad, who was tasked with making a quick check before we leave, in case anything has developed with Darcy that we need to know about.

'No. Still the same,' Dad replies, which is good news really, because it means my sister has still not been caught. The longer this goes on, the more resourceful we're all proving ourselves to be, although each day seems to bring a new challenge and, right here, we're facing our next one.

'Adrian and I will go first with the bags,' Karl says, nodding at my father, who is ready to move. 'We'll get everything inside, and then you guys quickly follow. Okay?'

My mother and I nod while Campbell watches his grandfather and daddy pick up the luggage before they step outside, leaving me to pray that Travis is not looking over at our cabin now. Even if he is, the darkness will hopefully mean he can't see exactly what's going on.

We wait for twenty seconds to give the men time to do what they said they would do before I tell Mom it's time for us to follow. We go outside too, feeling the chill in the air now that it's nighttime. I look towards the car and see two silhouettes moving in the shadows, one at the trunk loading luggage while the other is getting in behind the wheel. I figure Karl is on bag duty while Dad is about to start the engine, though he knows to wait until we're all seated inside with the doors locked before he goes ahead and makes that noise.

I lead Campbell to the car, whispering for him to be quiet, even though he is already being so, but I need to reinforce it just in case he suddenly makes a sound that attracts Travis's attention. I glance over at the cabin in the distance as we pass it, but while I see a single light on in there, there is no sign of movement or anybody at the window watching.

'Get in,' I urge Campbell, but again in a whisper, and my son wearily gets in, possibly too tired to argue, or just wanting to get comfortable again so he can rest his head. I'll happily let him sleep on my shoulder once we're on the road, but we're not there yet. Although we're not far off as Karl closes the trunk as quietly as he can, showing that our luggage is now packed.

We all take our seats and close our doors with as little noise as possible before Dad braces himself to ignite the engine. We're sure Travis will hear this, but it'll hopefully be too late for him to do anything about it by then. As Dad goes for it, I tell myself that we're safely locked in here now and we'll be moving any second.

Then the engine fails.

Dad frowns and turns the key for a second time but gets the same result. No power. So he tries again. And again. By the fifth time, we all know for sure that something is very wrong with the car.

'What's going on?' I ask, getting more worried with each turn of the key.

'I don't know. It's not starting,' Dad replies, stating the obvious, as if I didn't know we're still very much sitting ducks stranded out here in the wilderness with a known murderer nearby.

'But how can that be?' I press him, wondering if it's more something my father is doing wrong than something with the car, because human error seems more likely than this reliable vehicle suddenly failing on us at the worst possible moment.

'I don't know!' my father repeats, exasperated. 'I'm going to have to get out and take a look under the hood.'

'I'll help,' Karl says. The two men go to get out, but that doesn't reassure me. I'd rather we all stayed in here with the doors locked and figured it out without anybody going back outside.

'Try again,' I ask, and Dad does give it one more go, but still no luck, and they get out. I'm left on the backseat with my son, my mother and one very paranoid thought starting to rattle around in my head.

What if this isn't just bad luck?

What if Travis has tampered with our car to stop us leaving?

I try to tell myself that such a thing is impossible. How would he have done that? When would he have had the chance? The other part of my brain, the scarier part, tries to answer those questions.

He could have done it last night while we were sleeping. He could have even done it today while we were holed up in the cabin packing our things. The main thing is, he could have done this.

So why?

As I watch Dad lift the hood, which now obscures him and my husband from view as they look under it, the sense that this is much more than simple car trouble increases, until I'm convinced Travis had something to do with it.

What can I do? If I say anything, I could panic my son and mother. I also don't want to panic the two men because they are busy trying to fix the issue, so they don't need me distracting them. That just leaves me to sit in here, feeling the cold creeping into the car and the anxiety creeping in alongside it.

The problem is, the longer we're stuck here, the more time there is for that man to hurt us.

Wherever he is, lurking in these dark woods.

TWENTY-SEVEN

DARCY

I appreciate absolutely everything Cody has done for me so far, but, perhaps most of all, I appreciate the fact that he has done as I asked and contacted Professor Wright to set up a meeting. The professor has no idea that I'm behind the meeting request, so as far as he knows this is just something to do with work. That's why I'm hoping he's going to turn up at this meeting place, outside a bar on a quiet street.

Cody messaged Professor Wright, saying he was struggling with lecturing and needed some advice from somebody who was good at it, playing to the professor's ego. The fact he suggested the two of them go for a drink only increased the chances of success, because Professor Wright does love a tipple. So, as I watch Cody waiting outside the bar, I'm confident Professor Wright is going to make an appearance any minute.

I'm hiding out of view in case he does arrive, so that he won't know something is wrong until it's too late for him to leave. I loiter behind a parked car. I'm more than ready to spring out of my hiding place and confront the professor. I just have to bide my time.

While I do that, I remind myself how he threatened to have me kicked out of medical college, and the apparent ease with which he was willing to throw away my entire career just to keep himself safe. It's terrible, though I've also considered what life might have been like if I had ignored his warning and reported what he did to Taylor to the authorities. Maybe there would have been issues for me if I wasn't believed, and maybe I never would have become a nurse, but would that have been a bad thing? Maybe I was destined to do something else, because being a nurse has been a disaster. I can't help but feel like Taylor might still be alive if I had taken her side all those years ago too. Whatever happens next, I'm still going to carry guilt over that, even if I can somehow bring Professor Wright to justice.

A taxicab suddenly pulls up outside the bar. When the door opens, I see the professor getting out. He's wearing a smart shirt and jeans, clearly having made the effort to dress well tonight. I wonder if it's for the benefit of any ladies who might be out drinking this evening in his vicinity. I bet he would love to get talking to an attractive member of the opposite sex and tell her all about how he's a bigshot professor at a major medical college and then dazzle them with his big brain full of knowledge. He seems that kind of guy. If that doesn't work, he might resort to telling them an anecdote about how he once taught me, the infamous woman on the news, because that might pique their interest and keep the conversation going long enough for him to invite them back to his place for a drink.

It sends a shiver down my spine to think of this man potentially charming somebody after what he did to Taylor, and who knows what else he's done in his past that might be even worse? That's why I'm determined to stop him, even though it might seem, on the face of it, that I have far bigger problems in my own life to deal with. And I'm still convinced that Professor

Wright could trigger more flashbacks from the past. But without any clue where my family are, and with nowhere else to turn without Cody's help, it feels like there isn't much I can do. So setting right a previous wrong is what I'm focusing on now.

I watch as Cody approaches Professor Wright and shakes his hand, thanking him for coming, as the pair of us agreed he would do to maintain the illusion a little longer. The next thing Cody and I discussed was him suggesting that they try another bar a little further down the street instead of the one they're right outside. That's the ploy that will be used to get Professor Wright somewhere quieter than here, where I can pop out and surprise him, but it depends on the professor agreeing to delay his first drink for a few more minutes yet.

He doesn't seem to object to Cody's suggestion, and the two colleagues start walking away down the street, allowing me to creep out of my hiding place and follow behind them at a safe distance, my cap and the arrival of nighttime keeping me well shielded should anybody else appear. As they go, I can hear the low voices of the two men, although not clearly enough to make out what each of them are saying. I wonder if they are talking about me, about the chaos at the campus yesterday and throwing around a few theories as to where I might be lurking now. If only the professor turned around and looked, then he would see that I'm actually right behind him, but he has no reason to do that, so he keeps walking to a quieter, darker section of the street, well away from those who are drinking in the bar.

Then Cody stops, just as we planned for him to do, and, with no one else around, this is the perfect place.

I hear the professor ask Cody what he's doing, but I keep walking towards them, and he must hear my footsteps approaching because he suddenly turns. When he sees me, his eyes go wide.

'Darcy,' he says as he acknowledges my arrival, and I get a

sense of satisfaction from seeing how shocked he is to have come face to face with me again. But this time is very different to the last time because, unlike then, I have the upper hand.

'You tricked me,' I say, getting right to the point. 'You told me you were going to get me some food, but you locked me in your office and called the police. And I know why. It's because you didn't want me to remember what you did. But it's too late, because I remember it. I remember it all.'

Professor Wright listens to my spiel before looking at Cody, no doubt realising that his colleague was part of this set-up too. So all he can do is laugh.

'So you've been helping her, have you?' he says to Cody with a shake of the head. 'I did wonder how she'd been able to get off campus without being caught. Now I have my answer.'

Cody chooses not to say anything, either because he's too nervous or because he respects that this is my time to say what I have to say to the professor.

'Like I said, I remember everything,' I repeat, refocusing his mind back onto me.

'This is ridiculous. What are you talking about?' he tries lamely. 'I have absolutely no idea what is going on here, but I do know how many people are looking for you, so, if I was you, I would get out of here before somebody sees you.'

Ah, what a gentleman. Always thinking of others before himself. Too bad I'm no longer blind to who he really looks after.

'You assaulted Taylor back when we were students, and I caught you. Then you threatened us both to keep it quiet, so she killed herself, and I guess I was too afraid of you to report it. But unlike then, I have nothing to lose now, so the truth is going to come out, and Taylor's family is going to get some justice after all these years.'

'Assault?' the professor scoffs. 'Darcy, please. Okay, so I called the police, but only because I'm worried about you.

You're suffering from a serious brain injury, and you have done some bad things, so I just want you to get the help you need before you or anybody else gets hurt.'

'Stop pretending to give a damn about anyone but yourself!' I cry. 'I know the man you really are, and I'm going to make sure everybody else knows it too!'

The professor stops feigning surprise and suddenly gets very serious.

'Even if you could remember something,' he says, almost hinting that he's guilty, but not quite saying it, 'who the hell would believe you? You're a deranged killer on the run with every cop in Chicago looking for you. Do you really think anybody is going to trust your word over me, a respected professor with years of esteemed service? If so, you're even crazier than the media make you out to be.'

He's trying to make me doubt my plan, but it'll take more than some nasty words from him to do that. Then he says something that catches me off-guard.

'Even if you did say something, it wouldn't be the first time you had,' he tells me. 'Years after you graduated, the college received an anonymous accusation against me. Somebody said I'd assaulted a student and needed to be investigated. Nothing came of it, but I know that must have been you.'

That's news to me, but it does make me relieved to know that I didn't just keep the terrible secret inside me once I'd moved on to being a nurse. I must have tried to get Professor Wright caught, though it obviously didn't work. And I mustn't have wanted to risk too much myself, which is why I did it anonymously. Except now he's said that, he's already been accused and nothing happened, why would this time be any different?

'I won't be anonymous this time,' I say, trying to counter it. 'I will be able to give more detail. I'll make sure something happens to you. I'll make sure you're finally caught so you can't hurt any more of your students.'

'What do you want me to say? That I tried it on with Taylor? Okay, I did, but only because she was always flirting with me. How was I to know that when it came time for us to be alone together she would suddenly change her mind and not want to sleep with me? And how the hell was I supposed to know she would get so upset by it all that she would kill herself?'

'She killed herself because you assaulted her!' I cry, fighting for that poor woman, because she is no longer here to do so for herself.

'What do you want me to do about it now? I can't turn back the clock,' Professor Wright says coldly, as if he has long since moved on from that incident that tore Taylor's family apart. But I haven't, particularly as I get a brief flashback of Taylor's mother, weeping as she stands beside her husband, thanking all the students on campus for the flowers and condolences they've offered since the tragic event.

'I bet she wasn't the only student you did that to,' I say. 'I bet there were others. I know what kind of man you are, and I'm going to make sure everyone else knows it too. Even if you don't go to prison, your reputation will be ruined. I'll see to that.'

'And you think that will help you?' Professor Wright snaps back. 'Or have you considered how it would just make things worse for yourself?'

'Worse for myself?'

'You don't remember the part where you tried to kill me?' the professor says smugly. 'How convenient that you would forget that part of the story.'

'What are you talking about?' Cody asks, beating me to the question.

'You put a pillow over my face and tried to suffocate me,' Professor Wright tells us, suddenly making that flashback make sense. 'You said that I was evil and deserved to die. But you stopped at the last minute and, when you did, I told you that you'd just done the right thing. Why waste a perfectly good future by killing me? You had so much potential, Darcy. I told you that all you had to do to realise it was leave me alone. So you did.'

I'm struggling to take that in, and the professor capitalises on my silence by speaking again.

'I told you not to ruin your future and you listened to me,' he says calmly. 'So I'll tell you the same thing again now. You're still a free woman. You haven't been caught yet, and maybe you won't be. So go now. Leave Chicago and, who knows, maybe the police will never catch up to you. You could live the rest of your life somewhere far away from here. But only if you leave. So what are you waiting for?'

He makes it sound so good. So easy.

Just leave. Forget the past. Don't do the right thing. Take the easier option.

The problem is, I feel like I've spent my whole life living that way, and this is where it's got me.

But do I have the energy to fight on? Or should I do as he's telling me and just go?

'Come on,' I say quietly to Cody, and Professor Wright nods his head when he sees that I'm ready to walk away.

I say nothing more to the man as Cody follows me. Once we're back in his car, I don't even care what the professor does next. All I care about is if Cody got what I asked him to.

'Did it record it all?' I ask him, and he checks his phone before confirming that it did just capture that entire conversation.

'I got it,' Cody tells me nervously. 'But are you sure about giving this to the police after what he just said? You tried to kill him?'

'I want him to face justice,' I say. 'And to make it right for Taylor. Don't worry about me.'

That seems easier said than done for Cody, but before he can drive us out of here, I have one more favour to ask.

'There's something else I need you to do for me,' I tell him. 'Just one thing, and then this will all be over. I promise.'

This time, I'm not lying.

TWENTY-EIGHT

PIPPA

We're still stuck in the car, not going anywhere. I'm still afraid that we're in danger. I look out of the window again but it's almost total darkness out there, except for the light I can see in the cabin in the distance. Dad and Karl are still looking under the hood to try and figure out what the problem with the engine is, but they don't seem to be having any luck, as they haven't joined us back inside here yet. Meanwhile, Campbell is getting restless, and I can't blame him because it's very cold in here. The temperature will only continue to drop if we don't get some power to the vehicle soon.

'I want to go back inside,' Campbell says, clearly preferring the cabin we just left over being out here. But going back is not an option, or at least I hope it isn't. I'm still intent on us getting away from that dangerous man in the cabin, but that all hinges on this car working properly. I decide to go out and check on what the holdup is.

'Just wait here,' I tell my son, before looking at Mom to make sure she knows to stay with Campbell and keep him occupied. Then I get out, not eager to leave the car, but certainly eager to know what the problem might be.

'What is it?' I ask Karl as he stands beside the front of the vehicle, while Dad looks closer beneath the hood with the use of a flashlight.

'I don't know, it doesn't make any sense,' Karl grumbles as Dad keeps looking. I really want him to hurry up, but decide not to say anything as that probably won't help. But, when I look back to Karl, I notice something.

The light in the cabin in the distance has gone out.

It could just mean that Travis has gone to bed, but as I look all around I feel like that's not the case. Then I'm reminded of the awful feeling that he might be the reason for our sudden car trouble.

'What if this was him?' I say to my husband. 'Travis. What if he's messed with the car so we can't get away?'

I'm almost hoping Karl shuts down that wild theory right away, but he says nothing, and things only get worse when Dad lifts something up.

It's a cable.

And it's been cut in half.

The unspoken words between us say that this is definitely proof of human tampering. I hear movement behind me, and my entire body turns cold. Looking over my shoulder, it's dark, but I can still see something approaching.

Or rather, someone.

It's Travis.

And he's carrying his gun.

'He's coming!' I cry, unable to keep my voice down, but Karl quickly takes hold of me and looks me in the eye.

'Get Campbell and your mother and get back inside the cabin,' he tells me firmly. 'Lock yourself in the bathroom and don't open the door again unless I or your father tell you it's safe to do so.'

'No, come with us!' I plead, not wanting to leave either of them out of here, but Karl pushes me away. I know we're running out of time before Travis reaches us, so I fling the car door open and do as my husband says.

'Come on! We need to go, right now!' I cry, urging my mother and son off the backseat. As they get out, I take Campbell's hand and start running, telling my mother to follow quickly.

As I sprint for the cabin, I look back and see Travis is still slowly walking towards our car. His pace of movement is unnerving compared to how fast I'm going. I also see Karl and my father stepping towards him, their hands out in front of themselves, confronting him, but what will happen if he doesn't stop?

My first priority has to be to get my son to safety, so I burst back into the cabin and instruct him and my mother to get into the bathroom.

'What about Daddy?' Campbell asks, but I just herd him into the bathroom along with my mother, before slamming the door shut behind us and locking it, as Karl told me to do. I hate to leave him out there, but I have to accept that he and my father stand more of a chance of fending off whatever Travis is about to do than the three of us would. But now we're inside, without any way to see what is going on outside, I'm starting to regret running in here. Maybe we all should have stayed and fought together? Or maybe we should've run further.

I start to think about unlocking the door again, although only I would leave the bathroom. I could keep Mom here with Campbell while I go to try and help the men. But is that too big of a risk? What if Travis has the upper hand and, once this door is unlocked, he has the opportunity to get in here and hurt us too?

'They'll be okay,' I say as both Campbell and Mom start to cry. But the waiting without knowing for sure is unbearable. By the time we reach ten minutes, I have to go and find out what's happening out there.

'Stay here and lock the door behind me as soon as I'm gone,' I say, but Campbell grabs my hand, not wanting me to leave, while Mom is reluctant too.

'No, you stay here and I'll go,' she says, as desperate to check on her husband as I am. I can't imagine she'd do better than me in a physical confrontation if it comes to that, so I pull away.

'I'll be right back,' I say before unlocking the door, temporarily putting us all at risk until I get outside and slam it shut. Then I only relax slightly once I've heard Mom turn the lock again.

With the two of them safe for now, I focus on the people who are not safe outside the cabin and move over to a window to look out. I can't see anybody in the darkness, so I leave the cabin, wary of being ambushed by Travis, but hoping he's already been dealt with.

And then I hear a gunshot.

The sudden, loud noise causes me to jump, but I don't make a sound because I'm far too afraid to do that.

Did that bullet strike one of my loved ones?

Have I just lost my husband or my father?

And what if the gun goes off again?

I want to call out for any survivors but I'm afraid. I run around to where the car was parked. I know I'm blindly entering a situation I have no control over. Then I see my father standing with his hands on his head, looking shocked, but at least he's alive.

'Dad! Are you okay? What happened? Where's Karl?'

I look everywhere for my husband, but I can't see him. I'm fearing the worst as Dad simply points past the car. I see my partner standing in the darkness.

'Karl! What are you doing?' I call out to him, fearing that he's vulnerable over there with Travis still lurking around. But as I go to him, I see why both he and my father are not panicking anymore.

It's because Travis is lying on the ground. As I get closer, I see something else.

He's dead.

I check on my husband, afraid he might have been injured during whatever happened, but he looks fine, albeit very shell-shocked.

'You're okay,' I tell him, as if he needed me to confirm it. He doesn't answer. He just keeps staring down at the body by his feet, leading me to ask the obvious question.

'What happened?'

'He came at us,' Karl says quietly. 'He aimed at your father, so I wrestled the gun from him. Then it went off.'

He points to the weapon on the ground nearby.

'He was going to hurt us,' Karl continues. 'All of us. So I had to stop him. I had no choice.'

'I know,' I tell him, not wanting him to feel any worse about what he's done, because I can see he is already incredibly disturbed by it. Then he finally takes his eyes off the body and looks at me.

'I'm sorry,' he says, which sounds ridiculous, until he adds some context to his apology. 'I'm sorry for everything I said since all this began. I know now that you were just doing it for our family. You were just trying to keep us safe.'

Karl gets it. Now he's been backed into the same corner that I've been in the past, he understands. There's nothing we aren't capable of doing when our families are under threat. This isn't the time for me to revel in a victory or say, 'I told you so'. So I don't do that, and when he throws his arms around me and hugs me tightly, I feel like I finally have my husband back.

TWENTY-NINE
DARCY

Cody has driven us across the city, well away from where we confronted Professor Wright. I don't expect him to have called the police again after our interaction. He won't be stupid enough to try that again, not now he knows for sure that my memory is returning, and especially not when he thinks he just talked me out of reporting him. But unbeknownst to the professor, Cody recorded everything that was said between us, so he hasn't got away with anything at all. But I'm okay with him thinking he has for the time being, though only until I put the next part of my plan into motion. For that, I require one more thing from Cody.

'Here's the place,' he says as he brings his car to a stop, and I look ahead through the windscreen to where he's brought me. It's a homeless shelter, and I see a line of people standing outside, either looking to get in or looking for some hot food. This is where I asked to be taken, wanting somewhere I can spend the night that isn't Cody's place. I feel he's already done too much for me, and I don't want to risk being caught there if anything goes awry with Professor Wright. This is a better option for me if what I want to do tomorrow is going to work.

'Thank you,' I say as Cody sits silently in his seat beside me. 'For everything.'

'It's okay.'

I suddenly get the urge to lean over and give him a kiss on the cheek. It seems to surprise him as much as it does me.

'What was that for?' Cody asks nervously.

'I just wanted to do it,' I say with a smile. 'Maybe I should have done it a long time ago.'

I have no idea how things are going to play out from here, but I do know that Cody has strong feelings for me that he's harboured for years, so I thought I better at least give him a kiss in case I never see him again after tonight. The feelings I have towards him have been growing stronger since we reunited, and I'm praying that, somehow, there is a way the two of us can be together again when all of this is over.

'So you know what you need to do?' I ask him, returning my mind to business.

'Yep,' Cody confirms confidently.

'Thank you,' I say again, though I really can't say it enough.

'You really think it will work?' he asks me, sounding unsure himself.

'It's worth a try,' I reply unconvincingly. 'If not, I'll hand myself in to the police tomorrow night, if they haven't caught me by then. But I want to give this a go. You understand, right?'

Cody nods and I think about kissing him again, this time on the lips. I don't, either because I'm too shy to do so or because I know I really should get moving so we can both go and do what we need to do.

The moment passes and then I decide it's time.

I get out of the car and start walking towards the shelter, keeping my head down beneath Cody's cap while pulling Cody's jacket tightly around myself, just trying to fit in as best I can with all the people already gathered here. Like them, I'm just looking for somewhere safe to spend the night and, like them, I am down on my luck, so maybe it won't be as hard to fit in as I expect. There is the possibility that one of these people recognises me from the news, although I'm hoping that, even if they do, they have bigger problems to worry about than reporting me.

I take my place in the queue before looking back over my shoulder. I see Cody's car driving away, and I feel my stomach lurch because I know exactly what he's driving away to go and do, and there is a second of panic when I fear it might not be the right thing. It's too late because he's gone and I have no way to call him off, though I eventually calm down and tell myself that I don't even need to do that. It's the best plan I have.

The queue moves steadily forward until I make it to the front, where I'm met by the friendly face of a volunteer who doesn't even ask me why I'm here, only if a blanket and pillow is enough for me this evening.

'Yes, thank you,' I say, appreciating what I am given, as well as the fact that I don't seem to have been recognised, which is probably partly down to the low light in this shelter and the cap on my head, as well as having wrapped the jacket firmly closed around my nurse's uniform.

I take my blanket and pillow and find myself a space in the large hall, where dozens of other people of varying ages are already set up, and then I try to make myself as comfortable as possible. If I can just get a couple of hours' sleep, that will be better than nothing, plus I don't expect to get much more than that anyway, on account of knowing everything that's likely to happen in the morning.

I've lain down on the gym mats that have been laid out over the hard floor, before pulling my blanket over myself and preparing to settle on my pillow, when I hear coughing nearby. It's repeated several times, so I look over to see a young girl with a woman who I presume is her mother. The girl is coughing again while the parent looks concerned, and I wonder if she's suffering from some kind of cold or infection. The odds of that are high if she's sleeping in places like this. The coughing continues and I feel like I need to go and help, so I get up from my resting place and wander over.

'Are you okay?' I ask the little girl gently as her mother looks up at me.

'She won't stop coughing. I don't know what to do,' the mom tells me, worry etched all over her face, and the girl looks very uncomfortable too, exhausted, and like all she wants to do is sleep but her cough won't allow her.

'Can I just check for something?' I say, putting my hand out to place it on the girl's chest. Both the mother and daughter look nervous, and I smile to hopefully assure them that I know what I'm doing.

I hold my hand over her chest, feeling her breathing as she coughs again, and when she does, I get the belief that it's more of a tickly cough than anything caused by a serious infection. It's as if I'm operating on autopilot, sensing what to do, and now I have a good idea what to say.

'Next time you feel like you're going to cough, put your hand over your mouth like this,' I say before demonstrating. 'Can you do that?'

The little girl nods. It only takes a few seconds before she feels the need to cough again, so she places her hand over her mouth.

'Now swallow and hold your breath,' I instruct her, and the girl follows my order. 'Then, when you need to breathe again, breathe slowly, through the gaps in your fingers. Keep your hand over your mouth and think to yourself that you are not going to cough anymore.'

The girl does that and, so far, she hasn't coughed again.

'Now breathe in through your nose and, if that feels okay, remove your hand.'

The girl slowly takes her hand away and seems to be waiting to cough again. But it doesn't happen.

'It worked!' she says, excited to be rid of the coughing. Her mother seems thrilled too.

'How did you know to try that?' she asks me.

The truth is I'm not sure. It's as if it was an old memory from a former time, when I was caring for patients, using my knowledge and experience to make them feel better quickly.

'Are you a doctor or something?' the little girl asks me.

'Not quite,' I reply with a smile, before wishing them both a goodnight and going back over to my bedding. As I snuggle down, I see the girl doing the same thing with her mother. Soon, the lights will go out and we'll all hopefully get some sleep.

When I wake up, Cody should have done what I asked him to.

If he has, the media are going to have something new to report.

I just have to hope the right people see it.

THIRTY

PIPPA

I'm safely inside the cabin with my family, and the body of the man who threatened us lies outside it, growing ever colder on the ground while we try to get warmed up again in here. With the danger from Travis now over, we don't need to leave the cabin, at least not so hurriedly, so we've decided to stay for the night and reassess in the morning. However, I'm not sure how much sleep those of us who know about the body outside are going to get.

Campbell is the only one who doesn't know about it, so the odds of him closing his eyes and getting rest are better than ours, and that's exactly what happens after I've spent some time sitting beside him in the bed and stroking his hair. He drifts off into a peaceful slumber, one I would be envious of if I didn't love him so much. I leave him alone and go to check on how the rest of my family is doing. I'm most concerned about Karl, considering what he just did for this family, but I know my parents are shaken too, and I find the three of them sitting in the living area very quietly.

'He's asleep,' I confirm before anyone can ask, as I take a seat beside Karl and put an arm around him. He feels fragile, like something has broken inside him now that he's taken a life, and I'm afraid to tell him that, unfortunately, that will never be fixed. Having had to do the same thing when I killed Eden to protect my family, I know the memory of that awful event will never go away, nor will it stop returning to me in the quietest, darkest parts of the night when I can't sleep. But the thing that allows me to keep going is the same thing that should allow my husband to keep going now.

'You had no choice,' I say to him. 'You had to do it, and now it's done, we're all safe and still together because of it.'

'Pippa is right,' Mom says. 'You protected your son. You protected all of us. So don't feel bad about it.'

I know it's just words and it's easier said than done, but it's nice to have my thoughts backed up, and then Dad adds his weight to the conversation too.

'You were brave and you acted decisively,' he says and, unlike me and Mom, he actually witnessed what went on outside the cabin. 'I'm proud of you.'

Karl looks up at my father and clearly appreciates the sentiment. I pull him in for a hug. It's crazy, but after our recent struggles and feeling like we've been on the verge of separation for so long, could this be the catalyst for us to overcome our troubles? I'd much rather it hadn't come to this, but maybe it was the only way for my husband to understand why I've done everything I have up to this point, and he certainly said as much to me in the immediate aftermath as we stood over Travis's body.

'You should go and lie down,' I suggest to Karl. 'You probably won't be able to sleep, but just get some rest.'

Karl actually accepts that suggestion more readily than I presumed he would and gets up to go to the bedroom.

'I'll be in shortly,' I tell him, and when I do join him, it will be the first time we've shared the same bed since we got here.

I'll let him get settled first, and I watch him go before I look to my parents.

'You should try and get some rest too,' I say, but neither of them looks as willing as my husband was.

'No. I can't sleep after that,' Dad says. 'Nor do I want to. We need to decide what we do next.'

'Same,' Mom says, so I don't bother trying to convince them any further.

'What about the car?' I ask. 'Can it be fixed?'

'Not with the damage he did to it,' Dad replies. 'But his vehicle must be here somewhere. We could take that if we can find the keys in his cabin.'

'And go where?' Mom asks.

'That's the thing,' Dad says. 'I have no idea.'

I have no idea either, so I decide to break up this conversation by turning on the TV and checking the news. Maybe that will help drive our next decision. We haven't checked for any updates on Darcy in a while.

I scroll around looking for updates and eventually find a channel talking about Darcy, although they aren't saying anything we don't already know. They're still referring to her being in Chicago and spotted at the college campus yesterday, but nobody seems to have seen her since, or at least reported it, anyway.

'I hope she's okay,' Mom says tearfully, and I'm thinking it might have been a bad idea to do this after what we've already been through tonight. That's why I'm just about to turn the television off and go and get in bed with Karl, when a newsflash occurs.

'Breaking news. Chicago PD have called a press conference, and we can go live to police headquarters for that right now.'

I stop what I'm doing, as do Mom and Dad, grateful that I didn't turn the TV off, because it sounds like we really need to hear this.

It seems incredibly late for a press conference, so there must be some big news to report, and I hold my breath as I fear that it's going to be something about how Darcy has been caught and the search for her is over. Or what if it's worse than that?

What if she's dead?

The same thoughts must be going through my parents' minds too, and as the news feed cuts to a large room where a police chief stands in front of a microphone, I realise this could be a very awful experience for all of us.

'This evening, we were spoken to by a man claiming to have been in contact with Darcy Miller over the last thirty-six hours, and he has significant information regarding her motivations and her whereabouts. He has asked to speak to the media so he can relay a message from Nurse Miller, as per her wishes. Despite some concerns about its content, I will allow it to be read out because it seems to be the quickest way to bring Nurse Miller into custody quickly, and with as little danger to the general public as possible.'

The police chief steps aside, allowing another man to take his place in front of the microphone and, while I don't recognise him, he quickly explains who he is.

'My name is Cody Barber and I have a letter here from Darcy that I'm going to read out,' he says, and I glance at my parents who are both too fixated on the screen to notice me. *'First of all, to my family. I want to say I am sorry for putting you through this. I love you and I hope you can forgive me for what I have done to all our lives.'*

Mom starts crying, and as Dad comforts her with tears in his eyes too, I feel my own vision misting over. It's typical Darcy that she would be worried about us first before herself.

'Yesterday, I was spotted at my former medical college where I studied to be a nurse when I was younger. My reason for going there was because I had a flashback of a memory from that time and was trying to recall more. While there, I sought out the help

of my former professor, Professor Wright, only to discover he was not an ally. The reason for this is that I remembered what he did when I was a student.'

Cody seems to take a deep breath before reading on.

'I caught Professor Wright assaulting a student called Taylor Keys. She sadly took her own life not long after this incident and, when I tried to report it, Professor Wright threatened to have me expelled, ending my dreams of a career in nursing. I regret to say that I went along with this at the time, meaning justice has never been done for Taylor. But I am trying to change that now and, with the help of Cody, I have recorded a confession from Professor Wright that I hope will lead to an investigation.'

I'm shocked at the revelations, as I imagine anybody listening to this would be. All this time I've been worried about Darcy and imagining her hiding out somewhere, yet she's been on a mission to get justice for a former student?

'I'm sorry for the panic I may have caused on campus yesterday and I apologise to anybody I have encountered these last few days who may have recognised me and been afraid. I would not have harmed you, even if I had to pretend like I could. I hope you understand I was only trying to stay free until I was able to catch Professor Wright.'

Cody clears his throat before reading on.

'I also want to apologise for all of my actions before this that have led to both me and my family being sought by the police. I know I have done some things wrong, even if I felt I had no other choice at the time, and I am trying to make things right now. That's why my time for being on the run is almost at an end and I wish to hand myself in.'

I gasp at that news, shocked that Darcy would give herself up without a fight.

'As such, I wish to inform the police where I will be so I can be apprehended easily. At midday tomorrow, I will be in the west corner of Hutchins Park. That is my favourite park and I have

many happy childhood memories there, which is why I have chosen it. And, one more thing, I will be wearing my nurse's uniform, because I am still proud to be a nurse, just like I know my sister is too.'

Cody lowers the letter to let everybody know that he's finished reading it, and as the news reporters instantly begin to dissect the content of it and analyse why Darcy would do this, I turn to my parents to get their thoughts. Specifically, I'm curious if they noticed the same thing I did.

'She mentioned Hutchins Park, but that's not her favourite park, is it?' I say. 'That's not where we played as kids.'

'No, it's Greenwood Park,' Dad says, and I nod because he's absolutely right.

'Why would she say the wrong park?' Mom wonders, but I think I've already got it.

'It's a hidden message, just for us,' I realise. 'She knows there's a chance we might hear this, so that's why she mentioned her favourite park. She wants us to know that's where she'll be at midday tomorrow so we can have a chance of getting to her while the police are looking elsewhere.'

My parents look surprised at that idea but, the more I think about it, the more I'm convinced that is what this means.

'Darcy isn't handing herself in to the police,' I tell them. 'She just wants us to be able to find her. Or, rather, she wants me to. She mentioned me at the end. She was telling me that I'm the one to come and meet her.'

As my parents share a look, I leap to my feet, adrenaline coursing through me as I think about the task my sister has just set for me.

'I need to go to Chicago and get her,' I say. 'And I need to wear my uniform. That's why she said about how proud we both were to be nurses. She wants me to wear the same thing she is tomorrow.'

'Why would she want that?' Mom asks, and that's one thing

I don't have the answer to. There must be a good reason why, because my sister wouldn't have said it if there wasn't, and she's far too clever to waste words during a public message.

My sibling has just been smart enough to talk to me while making the police think she was talking to them.

That makes me think she must be smart enough to have come up with a way for the pair of us to get out of Chicago without getting caught too.

So that's why I'll take the risk.

I'm going to go and get my sister back.

THIRTY-ONE
DARCY

Despite my unusual surroundings and my even more unusual circumstances, I did manage to get some sleep. As I open my eyes and look around the homeless shelter, I see several people are still lost to the world of slumber, including the little girl whose cough I helped clear up last night. I'm glad she's sleeping well, although her mother doesn't seem to be. She's wide awake, watching over her daughter, presumably to ensure she's safe in this environment that is full of so many strangers.

I watch the parent and child for a few minutes, wondering what led them to be here, and finding comfort in the fact they have each other, before my own problems return to cloud my mind. Then I think about Cody and wonder if he's done what I needed him to do. There's only one way to find that out. I need to check the news, so I get up off my 'bed', collecting the blanket and pillow before carefully sidestepping the other sleeping people here as I make my way to the exit.

'Thank you,' I say as I hand back my bedding to the woman who sits on the counter, and she smiles as she accepts them, more focused on putting the linen in the right pile than looking at my face, which allows me to slip out still unrecognised.

It's a chilly morning and the sun has only just risen, but the city has already woken, and I can hear plenty of sounds from the surrounding streets. Cars, commuters and even a helicopter engine buzzing overhead in the distance tell me that nothing is ever quiet around here for long, and it certainly won't be today if Cody has done as I asked.

I make my way on foot to my planned destination, careful as I go not to be recognised en route, as that would really ruin the carefully laid plan. I'm also on the lookout for a glimpse of a TV, as I want to see the news and ensure that my plan is actually already in action. When I see a café up ahead, I wonder if they have a television that the diners can glance at during breakfast.

I look through the window and see a couple of people tucking into scrambled eggs and bacon, and beyond them, I see a TV screen tuned to the news, and the headline graphic across the bottom tells me all I need to know.

KILLER NURSE SET TO HAND HERSELF IN TO POLICE TODAY

I smile to myself, not because of the headline specifically, but because of what it means. Cody did as I asked him. He kept his word. I should never have doubted him. There's clearly very little that man won't do for me.

I only hope it won't all be in vain now.

I walk on before anybody can spot me lingering out here, and as I make my way along the city streets they grow progressively busier. It's not just the start of a typical city day that has so many people pouring out of the buildings. It's that there are two big things occurring in Chicago today.

One, the huge police operation that is underway as they surround Hutchins Park, which is where everyone falsely believes I am going to be at midday. And two, the large parade that is scheduled to pass through the downtown area at the same time, the parade that I saw being advertised on a poster yesterday, which gave me the idea of what to do today.

The parade is the other story dominating the local news and, as I pass another TV screen, I get glimpses of the large event that is coinciding with the police operation to take me into custody.

RETURN OF THE NURSE PARADE – Chicago set to celebrate nurses in revival of city parade that ran from 1949 to 1958

The news shows grainy footage of the parade that used to run through Chicago over sixty years ago, the parade that's making its comeback today. There will be thousands of nurses taking to the streets to celebrate. Most of them will be actual medical professionals, although many will simply be actors in costume, along with countless other people who wish to take part playing the role of patients. Alongside them, there will likely be thousands who line the streets to watch them all pass by, so it promises to be a very busy day for the police in the city, and that was before I announced my wish to hand myself in. Thankfully, the parade doesn't appear to have been cancelled, so that will be going on at the same time I'm due to meet the police in the park, ensuring their capabilities are stretched to the limit, which is how I want it.

As I keep walking, I hear more helicopters buzzing overhead, and see several police cars pass by me heading in the direction of the park. I also see several nurses in uniform making their way to the parade starting point, as well as a large float featuring a constructed hospital being manoeuvred into position.

It's all action, but as more police cars speed past and I watch one helicopter fly right over my head before disappearing behind a tall building, I take a left turn and start walking to where things seem quieter. Unlike all those police officers, I am not going to Hutchins Park. Instead, I am making my way to Greenwood Park, which should be much quieter, with almost everybody expecting me to be elsewhere.

I hope it's not too quiet; there's somebody I hope to see there.

When the clock strikes midday, I pray that my sister will be there to join me.

If she isn't – either she didn't see my message or is too far away to respond in time – I guess I'll take it as a sign that this should be over and I'll hand myself in.

But I'm praying Pippa does what I need her to do, because I don't want this to be over.

Not yet.

THIRTY-TWO

'Where are you going, Mommy?'

Campbell's question is an innocent one, laced with fear, as he clearly doesn't want me to leave him and, if I'm honest, I don't want to leave him. I cannot take him with me, it's too risky, mainly because I have no idea what I would be taking him into. All I know is that it would be no place for a child.

'You stay here with Daddy and Granny and Grandpa,' I say to him before giving him a kiss on the forehead. 'I'll be back soon and, hopefully, I'll have your auntie Darcy with me.'

'Really?' Campbell says, excited at the sound of his auntie's name, because he hasn't seen her in such a long time, and he always adored her.

'Yes,' I say, knowing it might be a lie, but if it makes him happy enough to let me leave without a fuss then it's worth a try. I feel bad though, because lying to our son is something I've held against my husband before, when in reality lies are sometimes a part of good parenting.

'Hurry back,' Campbell says after I've given him a hug. As I reach the door, I turn back and look at my little boy one more time, hoping it won't be the last. The truth is I don't know what's going to happen when I go to Chicago to try and find Darcy.

Maybe everything will work out okay.

Or maybe it will be the end of this family forever.

My next goodbye is to my mother, whom I hug tightly.

'Find her and make sure she's okay,' she tells me, and I nod to confirm I understand the assignment. I'm also relieved that Mom isn't insisting that she come with me, as it could have only complicated things in Chicago, and we need to try and keep them as simple as possible.

With Mom staying back in the cabin to watch over Campbell, I leave it and head outside to where my husband and father are making checks on Travis's car, which they found covered by several loose, leafy branches to make it less visible to any passers-by. With our vehicle out of operation, I have no choice but to take the car belonging to the man my partner killed last night. It's a vehicle that we presume is stolen, which will mean the police might be on the lookout for it already as I'm driving it back to the city. It will only increase the difficulty of my task, but there is no other choice. That car is the only way I have out of here. I reach the men and nervously ask them if it's roadworthy.

'It all looks okay,' Dad says to me as he closes the hood.

'There's plenty of fuel,' Karl confirms from behind the wheel where he's been checking the dashboard. The engine is already running after the keys to the car were found inside Travis's cabin, which didn't seem quite as nerve-wracking a place to be in now that he's dead. His body lies covered by more foliage so Campbell can't see it if he wanders off, while the gun has been buried deep, so it can't be found by anybody else who could come to harm.

I want to give Karl a hug before I go, but I embrace my father first. He has a similar sentiment to pass on to me about Darcy as my mother.

'Go get your sister,' he says to me boldly. 'Bring her home.'

I know this is not home, far from it, but to have Darcy here with us would mean we were a full family again, so that's what Dad is getting at, and I nod to him too, having now let both my parents know that I am going to stop at nothing to rescue my sibling.

All that's left to do is look to Karl, who, so far, has not tried to talk me out of going to the park in Chicago where I believe Darcy is waiting to meet me. I'm sure he would have done that before the incident with Travis, but, since then, he has come to understand the desperate lengths people can go to in order to save family members. He is no longer an obstacle to me but a pillar of support. I cling to that pillar now, squeezing him tightly and telling him that I love him as he says the same thing back before adding one more sentiment.

'Just do what you have to do to keep her safe,' he tells me. 'And yourself.'

'I will,' I assure him, as if he needed it, and with that I'm set to leave the majority of my family behind here to go and seek out the solitary member who's still missing.

I get in the car and familiarise myself with the controls, before giving a wave to those outside to let them know that I'm all set. Then I reverse away from the cabins before turning around and beginning the long trundle down the dirt track that leads back to the main road.

It's awfully quiet as I go, only the low sound of the engine for company, and by the time I reach the road I decide that I need some companionship on this drive, so I put the radio on. It takes a while to pick up a strong enough signal and, when I do, I'm able to get updates from Chicago.

'A large police presence is expected at Hutchins Park where Nurse Darcy Miller is believed to be willing to hand herself over to the authorities at midday today. But the chief of police is urging caution, as well as for members of the public to stay away *from the park, and cordons have been established to try and assist with that.'*

I'm emboldened by the fact that everything seems to still be going ahead as planned, which means Darcy has not been captured yet and everybody is still talking about Hutchins Park, which I am convinced is not where my sister is really going. It will be quite incredible if she's been able to fool everyone in the city, though I'm still unsure if we'll be able to get out of there without being seen. That is until I hear something else that tells me my sister's plan is even more brilliant than I first thought.

'There is certainly a lot going on in Chicago today, and it's not just about Nurse Miller. That's because today marks the return of the once annual Nurse Parade through the streets of the city, a tradition that began in the post-war period and has been rekindled to mark the outstanding work of the nurses and other medical staff in the state of Illinois. Some experts are saying this cannot be a coincidence that Nurse Miller wishes to hand herself in on the same day as the parade that celebrates her profession is scheduled, making it a possibility that she has chosen today because she does not wish to sully the name of nurses any more. As if she thinks ending the hunt for her today is a way to show her respect to her fellow nurses who, unlike her, have done nothing wrong, and represent their profession with the utmost dignity.'

I didn't know about the parade today, but now that I do, my mind is spinning. Like these so-called experts theorising on the radio, I too believe that it can't be a coincidence. Unlike them, I'm not so sure that Darcy has chosen to give herself up today to make amends for being a bad nurse on a day that celebrates them. I think she's chosen today as she knows there's a chance the two of us might have to make our escape on foot, and what better way for two nurses to disguise themselves than running through streets that are already filled with other nurses.

That must be why she told me to wear my uniform.

The parade is her Plan B if Plan A goes awry.

If I wasn't so anxious, I would laugh and even toot my horn at how creative my sister is – she really is something. I don't, though, because my nerves continue to get the better of me, and that becomes more the case the closer I get to the city.

It's a long drive, but I keep the radio on the entire time, the signal getting stronger the closer I get, while the butterflies in my stomach only strengthen the more I pass the point of no return. As the skyscrapers come into view ahead, I see two helicopters buzzing among them, circling the city, presumably zeroing in over the park where they think Darcy will be. I am driving to the other park, the one where I think she'll be. Traffic gets denser, many normal routes are closed due to the parade, and I follow the diversions until I see the park gates up ahead.

As I had hoped, and I'm sure Darcy did too, there are no police officers here. They're all several miles away, and the helicopters I see in the distance mark out the space between me here and them over there. If Darcy is in this park, she's played her hand perfectly.

But is she here?

As I park the car and make my way through the gates, I have no idea if my journey has just been a total waste of time or if I'll be able to make it back to the cabin where the rest of our family is waiting for us.

There's only one way to find out.

Please let my sister be here.

If not, I'll be all alone, and this could be the end for us.

THIRTY-THREE

DARCY

It's almost noon, not that I'd have to check the clock tower in the distance to know that. I could figure it out from the noise I can hear in the distance. Helicopters are swarming and sirens are blaring, but, crucially, it's all occurring at a different park to the one I'm in. That doesn't mean I can relax; as time keeps ticking by, two things will happen.

One, the police will eventually figure out that I lied to them and start looking for me elsewhere.

And two, the longer I'm here alone, the less likely it is that my sister might appear.

I keep looking around the park for Pippa while safely hidden in my hiding spot behind the trunk of this chunky oak tree, though I'm ready to step out if I do see my sister approaching. There's no sign of her yet, even though the clock tower chimed noon a few minutes ago now.

Did she understand my message on the news?

Did she even hear it?

Or is she not coming and I'm still going to be alone?

I've put so much of my hope into seeing Pippa again here today that I have no idea what to do if she doesn't show up, other than to wander out of here and keep walking until I eventually get spotted by a police officer. That's how close I feel to giving up.

And then I see her.

I know it's Pippa even though she's still far enough away for me to not be able to make out her face clearly. That's because I'd recognise her gait anywhere. The way she walks, moves, the length of her strides, the slight swinging of the arms and the gentle bobbing of her head.

It's her.

It's my sister.

I want to run out from behind the tree and call out her name, but I worry there might be a member of the public around and, if they hear me, they could alert the police. So I stay where I am and allow Pippa to get closer, watching her as she nears, her head turning now, looking in all directions, trying to spot me like I've already spotted her.

Just a little nearer. Just a tiny bit closer.

I cannot wait anymore and leap out of my hiding place before sprinting towards the first member of my family I've seen in a long time. When Pippa spots me rapidly approaching, she initially looks shocked, before she smiles like I already am.

'You came!' I cry as I reach her and wrap my arms around her, clinging on for dear life because, now we've been reunited, I never want to let her go again.

'Of course I did,' Pippa replies as I cry tears of relief while regaining the strength I was losing just by having this support now.

I notice that Pippa also got the hint to wear her nurse's uniform, but before I explain why that is, I want to squeeze her one more time so she really appreciates how much her being here means for me.

'How are you? How is everybody? Mom and Dad? Are they okay? And Karl and Campbell? Are they safe? Where are they?'

My questions come at Pippa almost as quickly as I ran towards her, but she doesn't seem worried or sad. Instead, she suddenly smiles.

'You remember us all now? You remember our names?' she asks me, and I nod my head.

'I read the notebook every day. But my memories have been returning more and more since I came back here.'

'That's amazing!' Pippa cries. 'And yes, we're all okay,' she confirms. 'Everyone else is at a cabin north of here. They're safe and well, don't worry.'

'A cabin?'

'It's a long story,' Pippa says, and the buzz of the helicopters in the distance is a good reminder that I'd be better off not asking for that full story right now.

'Thank goodness you're all okay,' I tell her. 'I've been so worried since I saw you all on the news. The police looking for you. You must have been so afraid, and it's all my fault.'

'It's not all your fault,' my sister says kindly. 'What about you? Are you okay? We've been so worried about you. At least we had each other, but you've been all alone.'

Pippa holds on to my arms as she looks me up and down, making a visual check for any signs of injuries or malnutrition, but I'm okay, considering what I've been through.

'I'm fine,' I reply plainly, not wanting to waste any time on her worrying about my wellbeing. Now we've made it this far, there's no time for that.

'We were checking the news for updates all the time,' Pippa tells me then. 'When we heard your letter being read out and you mentioned your favourite park, I just knew it was a coded message for us.'

'I knew you'd get it.' I smile, so happy it worked, but as another siren sounds in the distance, I'm snapped back into reality. 'We need to go. The police might figure it out next, or at least they'll stop focusing on the wrong park and start spreading out around the city again to look for me. So we have to get moving.'

'My car is just outside the park,' Pippa says, pointing the way. 'We can drive back to the cabin and then, once we're all together, we can figure out what we do next.'

That sounds good to me and it is definitely Plan A. As long as it works, I won't need to enact Plan B, which is incredibly risky and might not even work at all. As we sprint towards the car and I see it in the distance, I figure it's going to be fine. But just before we reach it, I hear a voice behind me that instantly makes me think whatever plan I have is ruined now. That's because, if I had been caught here, I anticipated it being by a police officer. But as Pippa and I turn around to see who just called out my name, I know it's not as simple as that.

It's actually worse.

The person who's caught me does not have the capacity to arrest me. They can do something more final than that.

They can kill me.

And as I stare into Professor Wright's eyes, I get the feeling that's exactly what he's come here to do.

THIRTY-FOUR

DARCY

'How?' is all I can say as I stare at the professor who did what none of the police in Chicago could do: he's caught me and my sister before we could escape the city.

'Hello, Darcy. And this must be your sister. Pippa?' Professor Wright asks with a satisfied sneer, as he eyes us both up and down. 'What's the matter? Surprised to see me?'

'Who's this?' Pippa asks me, still in the dark about the severity of who it is that's just stopped us.

'I'm your sister's former professor,' comes the curt response from the man delaying our escape. 'You might have heard about me on the news recently. I'm being investigated by the police thanks to the outrageous claims your sister made against me.'

'They are not outrageous! You're guilty of it all!' I cry, defending my position. 'I remember what you did, and now I've told the world about it, so you'll never get away with it anymore!'

'That might be right,' the professor says calmly. 'But if I'm going down, you're going down with me.'

He's intent on not letting me get away with ruining his life.

But what I don't understand is how he even knew I was going to be here?

'How did you know I would be at this park?' I ask him nervously, still assuming only my family could have deciphered my coded message.

'You're not the only person who's been remembering things,' Professor Wright replies. 'I remembered something from the past too. A conversation we had once after a lecture. It was early on in your student days, and you came to me to say you felt you were struggling with the workload and were worried you weren't smart enough to be a nurse.'

I don't recall this conversation.

'Do you know what I said to you? I told you that you were one of the brightest students I'd ever had, and there were no doubts in my mind that you were capable of becoming a fantastic nurse one day. I guess I was a terrible judge of character. Look what you became instead.'

'My sister is a great nurse!' Pippa chimes in for me, but that only makes the professor laugh.

'Oh, really? Is that why she's wanted for murder?'

There's no point trying to make this man see me in a different light, like there's no point in him trying to make himself seem better in my eyes. So while I appreciate my sister's gesture, I stop us from wasting any more time.

'I still don't understand how you knew I'd be here,' I say.

'I knew because of what we talked about next, right after you'd expressed concern about becoming a nurse. I told you that you needed to take the time to have a break if you were ever feeling overwhelmed with studying, and then I suggested something as simple as going for a walk in your favourite park.'

I still don't remember this prior conversation, but I'm starting to see how this seemingly banal discussion so many years ago could have come back to haunt me today.

'I asked you what your favourite park was at the time,' the professor explains. 'And you told me. You said it was this one right here. Greenwood Park. And do you know what? It stuck in my mind for some strange reason. That's why, when I heard your letter being read out on the news, the one in which you said so many things about me, I noticed when you said your favourite park was Hutchins Park. I knew it was a lie based on what you'd told me all those years ago. So I figured I'd come here, to your actual favourite park, to see if you were here instead. And look at this, I found you, and just in time too, by the looks of things.'

As a man who lectures people all day, Professor Wright is extremely comfortable with imparting his superior knowledge onto those who know less than him, and that's exactly what he's doing. But this isn't one of his classes. The stakes are much higher than a failed exam and we both know it.

'What do you want?' I ask him anxiously.

'I already told you. If I'm going down then you're going down with me.'

I realise then that I could try and argue with him, but it wouldn't do me any good. He's here to stop me leaving, and anything else but trying to escape is just wasting time. That's why I turn to my sister and say one simple word.

'Run.'

The pair of us take off towards the car with the professor in hot pursuit. We have a slight edge on him and we're closer to the vehicle, which is why we're able to reach it first.

Pippa unlocks it and we both fling open the doors. I'm hoping my sister can get the engine started before he reaches us. But we haven't started moving when I see the professor pick up a large trash can, and I fear he's going to throw it at us.

'Drive!' I cry as Pippa hits the accelerator pedal and we lurch forward. The trash can is launched in our direction and it hits the screen with a loud thud, cracking but not breaking the glass, though it would have been preferable if it had entirely shattered. As it is, the web of cracks mean visibility through the windscreen has been totally removed. Without being able to see where she's driving, Pippa can't safely get us out of here.

'Abandon the car!' I shout, making the split-second decision that we're better off continuing our escape on foot than in this unroadworthy vehicle, so now we open the doors we were so desperate to shut and get out of the car before the professor reaches us.

'Run!' I say to my sister for the second time in quick succession, though this time we're not running to a specific destination but trying to put as much distance between ourselves and our pursuer as possible.

We cross the road that runs alongside the park and dart down a narrow side street, but as I look back over my shoulder I see the professor is still on our tail. We have no chance to change course or go back without him intercepting us, which is problematic because we're running towards a wall of noise, though that might not be a bad thing.

We're not running towards the other park, which would be a disaster, as that's where all the police currently are, not to mention it would take a while because it's miles away.

We're running towards something else that is just as busy, but where we have a chance of staying undetected.

We're headed for the parade.

As I run alongside my sister, I realise this is the part where I totally abandon Plan A and put all my focus onto my Plan B. In this case, the B stands for 'blend in'. This is why I told my sister to wear her nurse's uniform and why I'm still wearing mine. As we round another corner and see the back of the parade ahead of us, we're no longer the only two people wearing such a uniform. There are hundreds of nurses, and if we can just catch up to them, we can hide among them, making it look like we're part of the parade too rather than the pair of runaway women that we actually are.

Can we get there in time to even try and blend in?

Or is the professor going to catch us before then?

I get my answer a second later, and it's not the one I wanted, as I feel one of the professor's hands clutch my arm and pull me backwards. Despite my best efforts to break free, he has hold of me and drags me to the wall at the side of the street.

As I slam into it, both the professor's hands are now on me and, terrifyingly, they are around my neck, squeezing my throat. I fight to save myself but he only strangles me more. That's until my sister comes to my aid with a bit of sibling defence. We won't let any man get the better of us.

She strikes Professor Wright across the head with her fist as hard as she can, and the blow causes him to lose his grip on me and stumble to the side slightly. That reprieve is all I need to go into attack mode myself, and now I'm hitting the professor too. Between us we're able to force him down onto the ground as he desperately tries to protect himself from the blows being inflicted upon him.

However, despite us stifling him, I know it will only take him getting back to his feet before he has another go at killing me or my sister.

I cannot allow him to get back up, whatever it takes. Which is why, as he sits up, dazed but still conscious, I push him to the side, causing him to hit his head on the edge of the kerb.

All I was doing was simply trying to ensure he knows better than to try and get up to attack us again. But such is the force of the blow that it renders him unconscious immediately, or at least I think he's unconscious.

Pippa bends down and checks him for a pulse.

'He's dead,' she says quietly, her voice only just audible over the noisy parade that's just around the corner from us now. Although that changes quickly when I see another float arriving on our street, bringing up the rear, and I realise what we've just done is about to be seen. I need to think fast. When I see the nurses coming around the corner in uniform, joining the parade, I know Pippa and I could potentially follow them, and nobody would know we weren't supposed to be a part of it.

But what about the professor?

We can't just leave him lying here in the street with blood pouring from his skull.

That's when I see that among the group of nurses there's a team of people pushing gurneys, upon which lie people who are pretending to be patients. They're acting injured or unconscious, lying horizontal on the gurneys and being wheeled towards where the crowds wait further down the parade route. They give me an idea, and when I see a couple of the gurneys are empty, I tell Pippa what that idea is.

It's going to sound crazy.

But either we role-play or we get caught standing beside a dead man.

'Pick him up. Quickly,' I say to my sister as I grab Professor Wright's arms.

'What?' she asks, losing us time we already don't have.

'We need to put him on one of those gurneys so they think he's an actor,' I say, hoping it doesn't sound as ridiculous as it actually is.

Pippa sees what I mean, and also knows that it's either this or somebody in that parade notices we just killed a guy, so without any more hesitation she takes the professor's legs and we lift him off the ground. Then we haul his heavy body to the parade route.

'Hey, sorry we're late!' I say, trying to make it look like we belong here, and one of the participants falls for it, passing us an empty gurney that we put the professor's body on. As we do, the volunteer even comments on how realistic the actor is who's playing the role of our patient, before he and another volunteer start pushing the gurney.

Pippa and I glance at each other as we get swept along in the parade now with little time to do anything but try and blend in as best we can. That's because, as we see the crowd up ahead, we know it's not just made up of members of the public. There will be police officers in there too.

So we better not do anything to stand out from the crowd.

THIRTY-FIVE

DARCY

A marching band up ahead of us is providing the soundtrack as the parade snakes its way through downtown Chicago, the trumpets, trombones and drums keeping us all moving in time, as well as keeping up the spirits of everybody involved in this long procession. On top of that, on the various floats that are part of this parade, each one has a person using a microphone to communicate with the crowd, either telling them which hospital the nurses they're with belong to or simply telling everybody how fantastic it is to see Chicago looking as joyful as it does today.

The thousands of people who have come out to line the streets and support the parade are lapping it up, cheering for those passing by. Pippa and I are just two nurses among hundreds of others getting the acclaim of the audience, all of us in uniform, all of us walking in the same direction and, as far as anybody knows, all of us belonging here. It's impossible not to feel like we could be caught at any moment, and that's because we're passing by the thousands of people who have lined the streets to witness this event. Any one of them could recognise us if they gave more than a passing glance, just like any one of the participants of this parade could turn their head and realise they are walking alongside two notorious nurses.

But thankfully, for now at least, everyone in the crowd is too busy cheering and celebrating the nurses that move by to pick us out of the lineup specifically, which is a relief. Likewise, no one in the parade notices us as they are all too busy waving to the crowd. I get a little more assurance that we're not standing out when I notice three police officers standing among the crowd, but none of them make a move in our direction as we walk on by in the middle of the parade.

As crazy as it sounds, Pippa and I are just two people on a street with thousands of others and, as such, picking us out easily would be like picking out that pesky needle in a haystack.

I also hear the sound of a helicopter overhead and nervously look up to the sky to see the aircraft hovering high above the parade, possibly just looking out for trouble or perhaps specifically looking for me. It's late enough now for the police who were at Hutchins Park to have realised that I'm not coming. I imagine all resources have now been sent out far and wide to look all over the city again, that helicopter most likely among them. But will they be able to pick me out from all the way down here? Surely I'm just an ant in this crowd?

At least I hope so.

I glance back and see two of the volunteers pushing the gurney with Professor Wright on it and, like everybody else here, they have no idea of the reality of what lurks among them. They are just playing their part, entertaining the crowd, pretending, play acting, giving the audience a thrill because this is a cool thing for them to be witnessing.

I notice a little girl at the front of the line as we turn onto yet another packed street. She is waving a small American flag and has a big white ribbon in her hair. But that's not what makes her stand out to me. Rather, it's the fact she's wearing a nurse's uniform, having clearly convinced her parents that it's what she wanted to wear today to make this occasion. As we move past her, I turn my head to keep looking at her, and it's obvious how excited she is to be in the presence of so many actual nurses. For her, nursing is still a make-believe game, which is why she is in such awe of the grown-ups who actually do this job for real. I imagine she won't just want to pretend to be a nurse forever and, when she's older, she might wish to actually be like all these real nurses. We're inspiring her, giving her a goal to aim towards and, most importantly at her age, filling her little imagination with hopes and dreams. She is far too young to know the reality of the profession, of how nursing is mostly long, exhausting hours filled with monotonous chores that are repeated with frustrating regularity. That's even before you add in all the death and distress that comes with the job. But she's at the age where it simply seems fun, to put on a uniform and go and look after somebody, give them their medicine and make them better, basically all the pleasant parts of the job.

That poor girl has no idea.

As I'm forced to move on along the parade, I look away from the girl and turn towards the person walking next to me. My sister is anxiously scanning the crowd like I have been, and I'm sure she's thinking what I've already begun to ponder.

How can we sneak out of here and get away without anybody noticing?

Even though it seems counterintuitive to be surrounded by so many people when we're trying to stay hidden, it's actually helping us because we really are like needles in a haystack. That gives me hope that there might be a way in which we can slip away, and nobody will notice us, as there are simply too many other bodies around to distract the eye. Then, when I see a gap in the crowd up ahead – a section of the parade route that's cordoned off because it must be an access route for vehicles – I sense our opportunity to get out of here.

'There,' I say to Pippa, just loud enough to be heard over the marching band and the cheers of the crowd. 'We'll divert down there. Just walk fast and keep your head down. Act normal. That way, even if anybody notices us, they'll think we planned to exit the parade there all along.'

Pippa nods to confirm that she's on the plan, and as the gap in the crowd gets nearer, I am more than ready to be somewhere quieter again. Despite spending so much time alone and isolated over the past few days, it's far more stressful to be surrounded by people.

The gap gets nearer and I'm just about ready to make a move when somebody speaks to me.

'Nice touch. That looks really realistic,' a nurse walking on the other side of me says with a smile. When I look down, I see that I have some of Professor Wright's blood on my uniform. This woman is totally oblivious to the fact that the blood is real and the person it belongs to only died a short time ago. What's more, that dead man is actually a part of this parade too. Before I can reply and pretend like the red stain on my uniform really is make-up, I hear a shout behind us and, as I turn around, I see something awful.

One of the wheels on the gurney carrying Professor Wright has hit something, causing the gurney to topple over and the body on it to roll onto the concrete, which instantly makes the two volunteers who were carrying it worry that they have just injured the poor actor. But they'll have far bigger worries when they realise there is no acting going on. As Pippa and I watch on in horror, we see people start to realise that the man lying on the ground is not pretending to be ill or injured at all.

He's dead.

And the scream that goes up among the crowd confirms that my sister and I are no longer the only two people who know the truth.

THIRTY-SIX

DARCY

We need to run now. There is no other option. More and more people start to realise there's a dead person in the parade, so the chance of exercising that option rapidly diminishes. Everyone in the parade route around us stops walking to look at the body on the ground, while all those nearest to us in the crowd start to surge forward for a better view too. There is screaming and shouting, and while some may wish to shield themselves from anything distressing, like seeing what death looks like, more people are eager for a glimpse, because that's simply the morbid-curiosity side of human nature on show.

The behaviour of the crowd is making it impossible for me and Pippa to squeeze ourselves through the dense mass of people around us, and I can see that my sister is starting to panic, though it's not claustrophobia that's causing her angst. It's the fact that several police officers are now pushing their way through the crowd towards where the body lies, which is only yards away from where we are, and she is quickly realising what I just have.

We are never getting out of here without being seen now.

I could almost laugh at the fact that, in a parade that

stretches for miles, it's my tiny little part of it that has become the centre of everyone's attention, because it's so typical of me and my life. I could laugh if only it wasn't going to spell the end of my time as a free woman, but it surely is. As more police officers come forward, I see one of them look right at me and then my sister. Once the split-second act of him recognising us both has occurred, he is no longer occupied with who the dead man is, and I guess that's because he's already figured out who killed him.

That's why he's now alerting some of his other colleagues to our presence here.

I look all around for an escape route, but it feels like the tall buildings on either side of this street are closing in on us. When I see the panicked look on Pippa's face, I realise I can't keep doing this to her. She looks exhausted, and afraid, and she's also away from her family, her husband and son, who need her but can't have her, because I've taken her on this crazy ride with me. This is all my own doing and, despite trying my best to delay the inevitable, I feel like this is finally it.

The moment I face the consequences of my actions.

However, in order to do that, I want everybody to know why I did what I did, as well as understand that my family don't deserve the hate they've been getting in the media, so I spring forward and pull myself up onto one of the parade floats.

Rising up above the crowd as I scramble across the float, I see several nurses standing on top of it who all look shocked at my sudden decision to join them. Some of them recognise me, some don't. All of them quickly get out of my way, and that's how I'm able to grab the microphone that was previously being used by a nurse who was talking to the crowd as they passed by them.

There's a loud screech of static as I put the microphone to my lips, which only serves to get even more people looking in my direction, and as the marching band stops playing and the entire parade comes to a standstill, it's as if time has stopped in Chicago. The only movement I see now comes from the helicopter that hovers above me. As for everyone on the ground, they are all very still and very silent as they look up at me and realise that here, at this nurse parade, they have just come face to face with the most infamous nurse in America.

I see a police officer apprehend my sister and several others surround the float and prepare to board, so I start speaking while I still have the chance. Several cameras go up in the crowd, all recording me, and I guess the size of audience this eventually goes out to will be even bigger than those gathered here on this street.

'You're all here because you have come out to celebrate the men and women who dedicate their professional lives to helping others,' I say as I look out at the vast crowd. 'And it's right that you've done that because these nurses you see all around you deserve to be celebrated. It's not an easy job, but they make it look easy, and without them many people wouldn't get the help they need.'

I see a police officer pull himself up onto the other end of the float, so I take a few steps away before looking back at the crowd, all of whom are listening with nervous tension.

'But as you probably all know, I'm a nurse too,' I say, still taking pride in that title, despite all that's happened. 'Even though you will have heard all sorts of things about me, I was a good one. I loved my job. I worked hard and I strived to do the best work I could. I cared for my patients, and I hope that they know that it was an honour to look after them.'

I still have everybody's attention while the police officer on the float with me very slowly makes his way closer. I maintain the distance – I haven't finished talking.

'I feel terrible to have brought shame on the profession that has given me so much,' I go on. 'Maybe I don't deserve to call myself a nurse anymore, and maybe I don't deserve to be among so many other nurses who are far better than I will ever be. I certainly know I don't deserve to be here with my sister.'

I look to Pippa now, who is being held by a police officer so she can't try and run. Not that she's attempting to, as she's too busy watching and listening to me. 'My sister, Pippa, is the kind of nurse I should have been. No mistakes. No drama. I always tried to be the perfect nurse, but that was never me. That was my sister, and I am so proud of her for that.'

I smile at Pippa, not the sad smile of a woman who is about to be arrested, but the smile of a woman who genuinely loves and adores her sibling. I meant what I said.

'More than that, I'm sorry to have dragged her and the rest of my family into my mess,' I continue, looking away from my sibling and at the police officers who surround her and me now. 'The media has made them out to have done all sorts of terrible things, but they're wrong. The only thing they are guilty of is trying to protect me, a family member, and is there anybody here who wouldn't try and protect a member of their own family?'

I look at the sea of faces and hope they understand what I just said. But more than that, I hope the police are understanding this.

'The truth is, I did it all,' I say, veering away from the actual truth, but attempting to protect the ones who have spent so long protecting me. 'My sister and my parents did not hurt anybody. But I did. I've taken lives and watched them be taken. I stood by as Laurence Murphy killed his wife, Melissa, one of my patients, and all because I was in love with him. When I realised how wrong that was, he tried to hurt me, so I killed him in self-defence. I also killed Eden too, my former colleague, because she knew the truth and threatened both me and my family.' That last part is a lie, but I'm hoping there is a way I can get the police to think I did kill Eden, which will hopefully take away suspicion from my loved ones.

I use my next point to try and drive that home. 'My family is as much a victim here as anybody else. They told me to stop, to hand myself in, and they were horrified when I ran away,' I tell everybody. 'But I was selfish and I tried to save myself. Anything my sister or parents did after that was merely because they still love me, despite everything, and wanted to keep me safe. It was also because I threatened them. I told them I would hurt them if they called the police.'

Another lie, told to hopefully absolve my family of as much blame as possible, though I'm sure the police will have plenty of questions for them. More pressingly, the police officer on the float gets ever nearer to me, and I have no more space to move, or else I'll fall off and into the arms of the police officers who stand below me. But that's okay; I'm nearly done here.

'I did it all, everything I'm accused of and more, but I am not a terrible person who used her position as a nurse to her advantage. I didn't want to do any of it; it was circumstances. Self-defence. Desperation. Fear. Confusion. The car accident I was in changed who I am, and made me forget so many things, but I was not entirely innocent before it and I have made mistakes. Mistakes that I'm finally ready to face up to now. All I ask is that my family can be left alone. They don't deserve any of this. Only I do.'

With that, I feel like time is up and, as the police officer reaches me, I show him that I don't intend to fight any longer. Instead, I drop the microphone before putting my hands out to be cuffed. The steel goes around my wrists, and nobody cheers at the capture of such a prominent criminal.

They all just watch in silence as I'm taken away.

As does my darling sister.

THIRTY-SEVEN

PIPPA

There is a video of me and my sister role-playing as nurses when we were little kids. The footage looks old and grainy by modern standards. It was shot on a 1990s camcorder and it's shaky because my dad was filming it while following us around the house. But it tells a person all they need to know about what made me and my sibling special.

We were clearly enjoying the game, wearing our little uniforms and acting like we really were saving people's lives. In the video, I have a plastic stethoscope around my neck while Darcy is holding a plastic syringe. Together we're roaming our house, though to us it was a hospital. Our imaginations were free to run wild, encouraged by our parents, and because of that you can see on our faces that we really believed we were caring for patients rather than just being two kids having silly fun before bedtime. Watching that video back, as I have done a lot lately ever since my sister was arrested, I note how often my father chuckles from behind the camera as he records us, clearly amused by his daughters and their game. I also note how happy my mother looks when she occasionally comes into view, spotted in the background as me and my sister rush past or, occasionally, when my father takes a moment to focus on his wife and capture her happiness too.

But most of all, I note something about me and Darcy.

She seems far more serious and assured about the task we are undertaking. While I keep breaking character by giggling, my sister acts as if she really is on a ward and saving lives. She checks the temperature of teddy bears and toys, pats their head, tucks them into bed and gives them an injection when necessary, in just the right place on their arms. Watching my sister closely as she plays, it's as if she doesn't see inanimate objects but real people, ones who are sick and need her help, and that's why she gets annoyed at me at one point when I laugh too hard.

'We need more medicine,' she says to me later in the video as she looks at a pink teddy. 'He is very ill. Do we have any more pills?'

Dad is quickly on hand then, passing Darcy a packet of jellybeans that she uses to 'feed' the teddy bear, as if these magic pills will make him feel better. It's a simple scene, no doubt similar to what might happen in other houses around the world when children are playing, but what is not simple is how my sister reacts when she decides the teddy bear is not getting better at all.

'He's really poorly,' she says, pain etched on her face as if it's real, as if she hasn't realised that this is make believe, so she could just decide he's actually better and be done with the game. Then, just before the camera goes off – and almost unnoticeable unless you really knew to look – I notice something upsetting.

Darcy actually wipes away a tear from her eye, as if she is imagining so hard that this teddy bear is beyond her help as a nurse that it's upset her and made her feel helpless.

I'm not sure Dad noticed that day when he was filming, nor if he and my mother ever noticed when they watched this footage back. I have noticed it when watching it lately, as a result of going through some old things at their house, and it has really stuck with me for one reason.

That one fleeting moment as a child shows the core of my sister's character.

She really, really cares about others.

That's how I know more than ever that she does not belong in prison.

However, that is where Darcy is, and that is where I will be soon, though not as a fellow inmate of hers. Rather, I will be there to visit her, alongside my parents, when our weekly access allowance is scheduled to begin again. The reason we three are not in prison alongside our family member is owing to the information we were able to provide about the whereabouts of the wanted killer from Canada. The fact we had encountered Travis at the cabin, and knew the whereabouts of his body, meant we had information that we could trade in exchange for some leniency. Despite what we as a family had done, there was a decision that the crime across the border was bigger and even more well known among the public, and with the trail on that investigation totally cold, we had the chance to solve it. By giving the information about Travis, we not only gave the poor loved ones of his victims some closure, but we allowed the US and Canadian police forces to cooperate with one another and both look good in the eyes of the public.

Before our visit to see Darcy, I have another childish game to play and, this time, I'm the giggling parent while my own son is the one participating in it. He's not pretending to be a nurse or a doctor or any other medical professional, because I feel like I need a break from that. Instead, he's being a chef, cooking me breakfast at his plastic kitchen playset, and as he fries me an egg in his little pan, I rub my belly and tell him how hungry I am.

While I might be exaggerating, I'm certainly not exaggerating how grateful I feel to be able to witness this simple yet special moment with my child. That's because I know I could very easily be missing this moment, as well as countless other moments in the future, if the police really knew the truth about everything.

But they don't.

My sister has seen to that.

When Darcy grabbed that microphone at the parade and started talking, I had no idea what she was going to say. But as soon as she spoke, I realised she was still exactly the same person she was back when we were young. She still cared deeply about other people. That's why she praised the other nurses in the parade and spoke about what a selfless job it was.

It's also why she was incredibly selfless, and deflected all the police's attention away from her family and onto herself.

Darcy admitted what she did, but she went further and took the blame for things she didn't even do, like killing Eden, for example. That was me – my fault, my crime – yet Darcy confessed to it and, with the police not knowing any better, they still believe she's guilty of that. My sister also made out like she'd pressured me and our parents into helping her and keeping her secrets quiet, as if we were afraid of her and what would happen to us if we didn't. In other words, she made herself out to be a monster, which is obviously not true, but it sure did alter the police's perspective when they were assessing what the rest of us had done.

We'd suddenly gone from being co-conspirators to victims of circumstance, dragged along for the ride by their criminal family member. With Darcy admitting to everything, which solved all the cases that were open, the police were happy to let me and my parents, as well as my husband, avoid prison, on the basis that Darcy was clearly the instigator of it all.

The police no doubt enjoyed the fact that the media made even more of a story out of 'the killer nurse', suddenly spinning us as the victims and amping up how bad Darcy was, because it made them look like they really had caught one of the biggest villains to ever exist in Chicago. I'm sure some detectives and officers felt like we had more to do with things than they were being led to believe, but there was no evidence that Darcy hadn't forced us to help her, nor any evidence that we hadn't felt like our lives were at risk if we disobeyed her. All we had to do was go along with this story in police interviews, which was difficult as it simply wasn't true, and we hated having to make Darcy seem worse than she was, but we also knew it was what she wanted. She wouldn't have done what she did at the parade if it wasn't.

Family is everything to all of us.

This way, we've stayed together as much as possible.

'Mmm, that's delicious,' I say after I have taken a 'bite' out of the plastic egg that Campbell has served me, and I rub my stomach to show how full it's made me. My son giggles, enjoying the game, which makes me smile, because I know how lucky we are to even be playing it. I could blame Darcy for throwing my life into disarray, but that wouldn't be fair. Instead, I choose to feel thankful to her for ensuring that I still get to be a good mother every day for the rest of my son's life. He doesn't have to visit me in prison, even though he should be, and it's all down to the person I'll be visiting soon.

'That looks good. Is there any left for me?'

I turn to the door of the playroom and see Karl standing there watching our son 'cook'. Campbell instantly laughs before serving up some plastic bacon to my husband, who makes as much of a pretence of eating and enjoying it as I just did with the egg.

As Campbell finishes the cooking and begins the very grown-up job of washing up, Karl sidles up alongside me and puts his arm around me. As he gives my head a kiss, I snuggle into him, enjoying how close we are now, not just literally in this moment but in every way possible. With all the drama mostly behind us, we have the space in our relationship to enjoy each other's company again. There's less of a reason for fighting and much less of a reason to keep secrets. Then there's the fact we actually bonded over how we each killed another person to keep our family safe. I suppose that's one secret we'll have to carry to the grave, but we can manage that. Rather that than prison, divorce and our son not getting to see his parents cuddle and kiss every day of the week.

I hear the doorbell and know who it will be before I even answer it. That's because it's half past nine in the morning and the doorbell goes at the same time every week.

It's my father and, while he's on the doorstep now, Mom will be sitting in his car on the driveway. They're waiting for me to join them before we drive over to the prison where Darcy is being held.

It's time to go and see the infamous killer nurse that everyone in America is still gossiping about.

But to us, she's just Darcy Miller. One of the people I love most in the world.

EPILOGUE

DARCY

As a nurse, I took pride in the fact that I was serving the community. I also liked being surrounded by other people who were doing the same. I suppose not much has changed there. I'm still surrounded by people whose work helps the public, although these days, the public service is about keeping dangerous criminals off the streets.

As I watch the prison wardens go about their business, I wonder if they take as much pride in their job as I once took in mine, or whether it's just a pay cheque to them. This is not a hospital and there are no patients lying in beds, just convicted felons in cells, counting down the days until their release date, and all the wardens have to do is keep watch on them. I think being a nurse is better, though I suppose I would think that. The problem is, I've lost the right to do my job, and even the right to walk down the street as a free woman. I've been incarcerated for six months now, living in this high-security, low-fun place, and it's nothing less than I deserve. People lost their lives because of me and, as I'm the last one standing, I guess I'm the one who has to pay. That's okay; I made my peace with it the moment I spoke into that microphone at the parade. I'm also comforted by the fact that my family remain free to live their lives on the outside, just like I'll be comforted when they come to see me very soon.

I'm due to be led to the visitors room where I will see my parents and my sister and get time to talk with them before I return to my lonely life in here again. I'm excited to hear what they've been doing, to discover if my parents have done anything fun lately or if my sister has another funny tale to tell about my nephew, Campbell. Of course, as eager as I am to hear how they're doing, they will be eager to find out how I'm getting by in here. I'll do my best to put on a brave face and say I'm okay, but it's hard to really be convincing about that, because nobody wants to end up in a place like this. Yet here I am, much to the enjoyment of the police and the media.

Everyone loves that the killer nurse is behind bars now.

Everyone but the nurse herself.

As I make my way to the room where my family will soon join me, I glance in a few of the other cells as I pass them by, though as always I regret it because all I see looking back at me are sad or serious faces belonging to other inmates in here. Bizarrely, some of them nod at me as I pass, as if they respect me and the things they've heard that I've done. This is an all-female prison, so I suppose the fact I've killed several abusive and dangerous men makes me a bit of a hero to these women, as well as some on the outside too. I get occasional fan letters from members of the public telling me that I'm not a bad person and I appreciate that. I can't say I appreciate the declarations of love or the creepy messages from potential stalkers, but not to worry, because none of them can get to me in here. I guess it's part of being a celebrity. People will always talk about me, and some will be obsessed with me and my story, with some even saying I'm an inspiration to them. Maybe it's better than having lived a quiet, uneventful life? At least I'll always be remembered and, sometimes, when I'm lying in my bed at night after lights out, staring at the walls of my cell and waiting for the luxury of sleep to come for me, I smile wryly to myself. That's because, despite it all, I did take three dangerous men out of this world. Lawrence. Parker. Professor Wright. They all got what they deserved, and that thought often cheers me up, just like I'm cheered up by the sight of my family as they enter the visitors room to see me.

I'm pleased to see that my parents look well, considering what they have been through, as does Pippa, who looks a little tired, but she does have a young child, so I guess it's more that rather than worrying about me that's causing her fatigue.

Smiling because I am genuinely happy to see them, I allow them all to take a seat opposite me, unable to hug each of them, as that's against the rules here, but happy enough just to be in their presence.

'How are you all? Are Campbell and Karl okay? What's new?'

I always ask the first questions, and my family has learned to allow me to do that because it makes me feel better than spending the first five minutes talking about myself.

'We're all well,' Pippa replies with a smile. 'Karl's good and Campbell is being fun as always. He sends you big hugs.'

'Tell him I send them right back,' I say, wishing I could see my little nephew, but accepting this is no place for him and that he'll be a grown man if and when I ever get out of here.

'Have you heard anything more from the police?' I ask nervously, always afraid that they might think my family had more to do with things than I led them to believe.

'No, nothing,' Dad replies quietly, so none of the wardens around us can hear. 'Everything's okay there, so don't worry.'

'What about you?' Mom asks. 'Are things getting any better in here?'

'Yeah, I'm fine. Keeping busy. The days actually go quite quickly.'

I hope that will make her feel better, but it doesn't work. She shakes her head and looks upset all of a sudden.

'It's just such a waste,' she says. 'You're such a bright, talented person. You should be out there helping people. You were such a good nurse. It's not fair that you're being left to rot in here when you could be doing good in society.'

'Mom, I'm fine, seriously,' I insist. 'I think we can all agree that it's for the best that my nursing days are over. You're right, I was good at it, but I stopped being so and that's fine.'

Mom wipes a tear away as Dad puts an arm on her shoulder, and I look to my sister.

'Speaking of nursing, what about you? Have you had any more thoughts about what you want to do next?'

Pippa was suspended from her job after recent events and, even though some of her colleagues campaigned for her to return, she had to accept that her hospital, or any other hospital for that matter, was unlikely to face the PR disaster of having her employed on a ward. So she left of her own accord and, as of her last visit, she hadn't decided what to do next.

'I'm still thinking about it,' Pippa replies. 'But it's been nice to have extra time with Campbell. He won't be young forever, and it's far more fulfilling looking after him than other people's kids all day. I've actually been thinking I might homeschool him.'

'Wow. From a nurse to a teacher. Who would have thought?' I say with a laugh. 'You think you can manage that?'

'If I can manage a busy ward full of sick children, I think I can manage one unruly but mostly harmless young boy at home.'

'That's my sis.'

I smile at my sibling, and she smiles back, our bond as strong as ever and, after all we've been through, I don't think anything could break it at this point.

'Have you had any more thoughts about trying to help out at

the prison hospital?' Dad asks, referencing something he suggested to me on one of his previous visits.

'I don't want to and, even if I did, there's no way I'd be allowed in the hospital,' I say. 'Not with my track record. Can you imagine the outcry in the media if anyone found out the killer nurse was back nursing again?'

Dad can't really argue with that, but even if he tried to maintain that such a thing might be good for me, the last thing I want is to be thrust into a caregiving situation again, even if I do possess the medical expertise to make it work.

As the visit draws to a close, I've been comforted to see that my family members are doing as well as I could hope for, and they appear a little happier than they did when they first walked in here too.

Maybe everything is going to be okay.

Not the way it once was.

But okay might be good enough for us all.

'I love you,' I say to my family as we part again, and I'm led back to my cell by a warden.

I'm not quite back there when I hear a scream to my left and, as I turn, I see one inmate striking another. It looks like a fight and it's not uncommon for them to break out. They're usually brought back under control pretty quickly too, but I realise this is different when several other inmates start fighting, and they aren't just targeting each other.

They are going for the wardens.

Understanding this is suddenly a very dangerous situation, I try to get back to my cell because I don't want to be hurt, nor do I want to be forced into having to fight back myself as I might potentially hurt somebody else out of necessity. It's not that I'm worried about adding time to my very long sentences for murder and manslaughter, and rather that I really, really do not want to cause any more pain to any more people. But before I can get back to my cell, I hear something that makes me stop.

'Help me!'

That's when I see an inmate lying on the ground, holding her neck as blood covers her hands, and I realise she's seriously injured and needs urgent medical assistance.

Looking around for a warden who could give that, I see that they're all preoccupied with the other inmates and, as an alarm sounds to signal that control has been lost on this prison wing, I know that this inmate's life is in danger unless she gets help right now.

Rushing to her and dropping to my knees, I quickly assess her injuries and see that she is bleeding heavily from her neck, so I apply pressure to her wound.

'Stay calm, you're going to be okay,' I tell her, though the truth is much murkier than that, because she really is losing a lot of blood.

'How do you know?' the woman asks me, fear in her eyes as more blood leaks from her and onto my hands.

What can I say to that?

The only thing that feels right.

'Trust me. I'm a nurse.'

A LETTER FROM DANIEL

Dear Reader,

I want to say a huge thank you for choosing to read *The Nurse's Mistake*. If you did enjoy it and would like to keep up to date with all my latest Bookouture releases, please sign up at the following link, where you will receive a free short story, *The Killer Wife*. Your email address will never be shared and you can unsubscribe at any time.

www.bookouture.com/daniel-hurst

I hope you loved *The Nurse's Mistake* and, if you did, I would be very grateful if you could write an honest review. I'd love to hear what you think!

You can also visit my website where you can download a free psychological thriller called *Just One Second* and join my personal newsletter, where you can hear all about my adventures with my wife, Harriet, and daughter, Penny!

Thank you,

Daniel

KEEP IN TOUCH WITH DANIEL

Get in touch with me directly at my email address daniel@danielhurstbooks.com. I reply to every message!

www.danielhurstbooks.com

 facebook.com/danielhurstbooks

 instagram.com/danielhurstbooks

PUBLISHING TEAM

Turning a manuscript into a book requires the efforts of many people. The publishing team at Bookouture would like to acknowledge everyone who contributed to this publication.

Audio
Alba Proko
Melissa Tran
Sinead O'Connor

Commercial
Lauren Morrissette
Hannah Richmond
Imogen Allport

Cover design
Lisa Horton

Data and analysis
Mark Alder
Mohamed Bussuri

Editorial
Natasha Harding
Lizzie Brien

Copyeditor
Janette Currie

Proofreader
Faith Marsland

Marketing
Alex Crow
Melanie Price
Occy Carr
Cíara Rosney
Martyna Młynarska

Operations and distribution
Marina Valles
Stephanie Straub
Joe Morris

Production
Hannah Snetsinger
Mandy Kullar
Jen Shannon
Ria Clare

Publicity
Kim Nash
Noelle Holten
Jess Readett
Sarah Hardy

Rights and contracts
Peta Nightingale
Richard King
Saidah Graham